THE SHRINES OF MANITOBA

THE SHRINES OF MANITOBA

Dark Secrets Shall Be Brought to Light

R. C. Jette

RESOURCE *Publications* • Eugene, Oregon

THE SHRINES OF MANITOBA
Dark Secrets Shall Be Brought To Light

Resource Publications
An Imprint of Wipf and Stock Publishers
199 W. 8th Ave., Suite 3
Eugene, OR 97401

www.wipfandstock.com

PAPERBACK ISBN: 978-1-5326-9190-4
HARDCOVER ISBN: 978-1-5326-9191-1
EBOOK ISBN: 978-1-5326-9192-8

Manufactured in the U.S.A.   MAY 20, 2019

This book is dedicated to the Lord who makes all things possible; to my husband who has always supported me; to my children, grandchildren, and to my mother who I will one day be reunited with.

A very special thanks is given to Wipf and Stock Publishers who words cannot express my heartfelt thanks for their professional and helpful staff.

My gratitude for previously publishing my other works cannot be overstated. I thank God for them.

Previously published by them are:

1. *Storms Are Faith's Workout: Preparing Christians For Spiritual Ambush*

2. *The Elfdins And The Gold Temple: An Oralee Chronicle*

3. *Charlie McGee And The Leprechaun: Life's Curious Twists Of Events*

4. *Faith's Journey Confronts Obstacles: Instructing God's Soldiers To Overcome In His Armor*

5. *Satan's Strategy To Torment Through Physical Ambush: Educating God's Soldiers Of Satan's Plot To Shatter Faith Through Sickness And Disease*

6. *Spiritual Shipwreck On The Horizon: Exhorting Christians To Contend For The Faith And Comprehend the Deceitfulness of Sin*

And we know that all things work together for good to them that love God, to them who are the called according to his purpose

—ROMANS 8:28, KJV

CONTENTS

Prologue

Normand Essex kneels in front of four multi-colored marble shrines that housed cement coffins. He is bent over with his arms curled over his head. His body is trembling as he begs God to give him a male heir. There is confusion and bitterness in his voice. He is angry with God and believes that all his troubles are His fault. God has treated him unfairly. He had been tested and there is no physical reason for his not producing an heir.

He is convinced that it is the hand of God working against him, for God has allowed the devil to curse his family for generations. But He still permitted all of his ancestors to have at least one male heir, whereas, he is sixty years old and childless. He looks at his watch, shakes his head, and gasps out several sighs. His appointment with Eugene must be kept; this was his only alternative. God had given him no option with the present turn of events.

As he straightens himself up, he carefully eyes each shrine that has a picture of a newly married couple in a gold frame. In front of each picture is a crystal coffin housing wedding bands. Behind each frame is a silver candlestick with a white candle glowing which creates the ambience of melancholy.

He carefully picks up each crystal coffin one at a time and looks at the inscription inside each wedding band. Gently putting the last crystal coffin down, he looks up, and again accuses God of being unjust. He takes one more glance at each picture and somberly blows out the candle. Before the last flame is put out, he turns on a flashlight and blows out the remaining candle. With the light of the flashlight, he slowly walks to the door of an underground cavern.

Normand opens the door, steps outside, pauses, scowls up at the sky, and raises a clenched fist. He turns, locks the door, and then covers the entrance with tree limbs and underbrush to keep it hidden. Before he gets into his vehicle, he turns, stares at the hidden entrance, and again blames God for his troubles.

1

Not Again

Anna Paquette stepped onto her front porch to read her morning paper and to savor the sunshine. When she looked at her Mulberry tree to see the chirping baby robins, her eyes caught sight of a moving van parked across the street. "Not again!" She said as she dropped her paper. "Lord, how many times do I have to endure new neighbors in that house? You know what I've gone through with welcoming new neighbors to that particular house. I'm too weary to suffer it again." She gestures with both hands. "I understand that You give whatever strength is needed for all things. But please don't ask me to befriend any more neighbors. You know that I still haven't gotten over losing Daryl. At least when Joan was here, her friendship helped me to carry on. You know that she promised to keep in touch and I've not heard a word from her." She exhaled. "Please help me to just ignore that house and enjoy this lovely morning that you have given me."

She took in a deep breath savoring the floral odors coming from her blooming lilac bushes. Savoring the fragrance, she stooped and picked up the paper. "Thank you, Lord, for the lilacs. I'll have to cut some more of them right after I read my paper. Their bouquet seems to cheer up the house. How Daryl always loved this time of the year when the lilacs were blooming. He'd fill vases all over the house for their fragrance." She gave out a heavy sigh, sat on her cushioned glider, and tried to read the headlines, but her eyes wandered up the paper and peered over the top towards the movers. "This is absurd," she said. "A young widowed woman of forty-four doesn't need this aggravation. Lord, please help me to keep my eyes from looking at that house. I am determined to disregard it. It will not have power over me anymore." She felt her body tremble as her mind waged the old familiar war. What was it about that house? What evaded her? If she could only put her finger on the crux of the matter, she would gain peace of mind. But instead of revelation, her thoughts were confused. Why does the house seem to sell about every five years or so? Could such a charming house be cursed? Why did each woman label herself as friend and never keep in touch? Was she playing the role of "Miss Marple" because she read too many *Agatha Christie* mysteries? That's what Daryl always teased whenever she'd mention her foreboding. Well, whatever the reason for her anxiety, she wasn't up to dealing with that house, especially now that Daryl was gone.

Anna fought to master her apprehension. What was she doing? It wasn't like her to let some nonsensical thoughts interfere with her personality. Besides, she'd always frowned on unfriendliness. Moreover, the Bible says that a man that hath friends must show himself friendly. Fidgeting with her wedding band, she glared across the street. "Maybe I should offer them lunch and make their first night's supper as I've done with all the others. After all, since Bruce and Amanda Martin left about eighteen years ago, I've greeted Henry and Lily Cromwell, Charles and Connie Fitzborn, and George and Joan Tyler."

She sat back and tried to read her paper. As far as Anna was concerned, businessmen who traveled too much are drawn to that house. Although she'd befriended all the wives, it was Joan Tyler who became a godsend when Anna lost her Daryl last year, and her hasty move to Atlanta was startling. But her promise to visit soon had cushioned the blow; however, three months, three weeks and two days have found no word from Joan.

Anna leaned back and closed her eyes. Her eyes quickly opened to the laughing and squealing of her neighbor's grandchildren playing with water pistols. Perhaps if the Lord had blessed her with children like the rest of her neighbors, she could ignore that house. She'd married young and gave up a career in marketing to fulfill her desire to be a mother, which never came to fruition. But children or not, she mustn't let that house get to her. She tried to calm the turmoil inside, when giggling from near the van caused her eyes to spring open and her body to lean forward. She watched as a young girl about five feet tall, very petite, and curly brown hair was talking to an older man. "Who's that girl?" Anna caught herself and sat back with a sigh. "What does it matter?" She was in no hurry to lose another friend. But the girl did seem young, quite youthful; whereas, the man, tall with gray hair, looked to be in his late fifties. "Lord, what if he's widowed? What if the girl missed her mother?" That settled it. She'd make lunch.

§

Anna carried a tray with iced tea, ham and cheese sandwiches, and apple pie. "Welcome to Hunts Grove," she said to the girl. "I'm Anna Paquette, your friendly neighborhood self-made welcome wagon."

The girl took Anna's tray and placed it on a nearby box. "I'm Katie Mathers," she said, offering a hand that felt childlike, "and the man with the notebook is my husband, Byron." She threw up her hands. "It seems strange saying husband. I've only been married for two weeks."

Anna felt a cold chill run down her back. Oh God, I pray that she's not married to a traveling businessman? What does it all mean? Why is the foreboding so strong? She forced herself to dispel the questions and smiled. "No wonder you're so bubbly; you're a newlywed."

"I feel like a little girl with her dollhouse," Katie said, clutching her hands to her chest.

Anna placed her hands on her hips, and her stomach tightened with laughter. "My dear, you can't be much older than a little girl."

Katie's emerald green eyes smiled. "I am twenty-four, but most people do think that I'm much younger. As a matter of fact," she giggled, "on our honeymoon, people thought I was Byron's daughter." She lowered her voice. "His wife died, and that's why I think he married someone much younger than himself." She paused, twirling a chestnut brown curl with the forefinger of her left hand, as her husband walked by with the movers. "Byron," she said, stretching her left hand towards Anna, "this is Anna Paquette, our new neighbor."

Before Anna could say a word, he gave a swift nod of his head, quickly turned around, and followed the movers into the house.

Katie watched her husband walk away. "He's very shy when it comes to strangers," her jeweled-eyes giggled with her, "which is so strange for someone who travels all over the country on business for a large pharmaceutical company. But he did say that he does it for the money and not because he enjoys it." She twirled a curl around her left forefinger. "He said that he's glad that he makes a lot of money so that I won't need anything. I am to buy anything that I want and not be concerned about the cost." She pointed to the house. "I never thought that I would ever have my own house. It is so beautiful, everything is just perfect." She gestured toward the roses. "The deep red roses are almost picturesque. The bushes are full of them. I am so blessed."

Anna listened as Katie praised the house and how much she loved the rose bushes flush with deep red roses. But her mind raced. Why another newlywed whose husband travels? Why are the husbands that move into that house always unfriendly? Is it a trait of traveling businessman? Did they tire of being sociable on the job and desired to be left alone at home? Katie did say that her husband does it for the money and not because he enjoys it. But still, what caused the ever-present foreboding about that house? No matter what she does, she cannot shake the feeling. She has prayed and prayed, but all the Lord ever says is to trust Him. She really must stop all this questioning. After all, what can she do? Maybe she should just forget about the house and befriend Katie.

Katie's laughing snapped her out of her thoughts. "Anna, I don't think you heard a word I was saying. You're just staring at the roses. Are you okay?"

Anna shook her head. "I am sorry, it was just that I was reminded of something. It seems to have taken hold of me. Please forgive me."

"Oh, it's all right. I find myself doing that a lot." She took a sip of her iced tea. "Thank you so much for these sandwiches and tea." She giggled. "Of course, I'm really looking forward to the apple pie."

"You enjoy it all." Anna placed her hands on her hips. "Well, if you don't mind, I'll cook supper for you both tonight. I know how busy you are with trying to move in."

Katie grabbed Anna's right hand. "Thank you so much. That would be terrific. This way I'll be able to concentrate on getting the kitchen stuff unpacked." She giggled. "It's all brand new. Byron wanted me to have whatever I wanted." She gestured toward the house with her left hand. "The boxes are already in the kitchen, so I'll be able to start cooking tomorrow."

2

THE PROBLEMS OF EACH DAY ARE ENOUGH

Anna sat at her gate-leg table with beautiful vase-and-ball turnings, opened the tin box that contained Joan's pictures in a small album, the note she left the day she moved, and the tortoiseshell box with a gold locket inside. She took the note and read Joan's promise to call with her new address and to visit soon. Anna placed the note back in the box and closed the top. Again, her mind whirled with questions. Why hasn't she been in touch? Where is she? Why didn't she keep her promise? She rested her head on her arms and wept. Through the tears, she heard what her grandmother said when she lost her mother at six. "Anna, remember that sorrow can be like quicksand that engulfs little by little. If you don't pull yourself loose, it will gradually smother the life out of you." Was that happening to her? She did feel overwhelmed and lethargic. Maybe she should really try to befriend Katie, but she couldn't bear to lose another friend. Besides, she wasn't sure if she and Daryl had pushed their friendship on the others. They both felt sorry for the brides whose husbands were away more than they were home. But now she wondered if they all felt overwhelmed by her and Daryl trying to help them not to be so lonely. Why else would they move away and never write? If they considered themselves a friend, wouldn't they have kept in touch?

The sound of Katie's voice startled her and caused her to jump from her seat. "Anna! Could you get the door?" Katie shouted.

She caught her breath, placed the box on the counter, splashed cold water on her eyes, patted them dry with a towel, and hurried to open the door.

"Byron left before dawn," Katie said, beaming up at Anna. "Since we're both alone, I figured it's time we got acquainted." She looked down at her tray that carried a percolator and cinnamon buns. "I made these from a new recipe. But after the meal you brought over the first night we moved in, I knew you're the best cook I've ever known."

"Come in," Anna motioned with her right hand. "Put the tray on the table and have a seat, while I get the cups."

Katie placed it down, flopped into a chair, and stretched her arms. "Phew! It was getting heavy." She perused the kitchen with its stainless-steel appliances, maple cabinets, the hutch, the table and chairs. "This furniture looks antique. Is it?"

Anna shook her head. "Yes, the table is a gate-leg table with tongue-and-groove joints of leaves and top with beautiful vase-and-ball turnings. The chairs are bow back Windsor arm chairs. She gestured with her right hand. "That's a Welsh buffet and hutch holding my special china and my grandmother's silver tea set."

"How do you know about antiques?"

"I've always been fascinated by them and have studied about them for years. You'll find that I have antiques in every room." She paused. "Many of them were my grandmother's. I suppose that's where I first became interested in them. I lived with her after my mother died when I was only six." Anna opened the kitchen cupboard and took out two cups, two saucers, placed a cup and saucer in front of Katie, placed one in front of the chair across from Katie, and sat down. "Oh yes, about my cooking," she said, as Katie poured the coffee, "I thank you for the compliment, but I'm sure your mother's a good deal better."

Katie put the percolator down and gestured with both hands. "I'm an orphan. I never had the advantage of a mother's cooking. So, I have no idea if my mother was or wasn't a good cook."

"I'm sorry," Anna said, feeling her face flush, "I never meant to bring up past memories that could be distressing."

Katie grabbed Anna's right hand and squeezed it. "I'm fine. It seems I've always had a faith in God that looks at the present." She twirled a chestnut brown curl around her left forefinger. "You see in the orphanage, we went to this little country church that ran the orphanage. The Pastor used to take extra time on Sunday afternoons to talk to any of us who needed to talk. He taught that although we had been abandoned by our parents, God was our heavenly father who loved us and was watching over us." She sat back with her emerald green eyes sparkling. "I figured if Jesus could suffer on the cross to save me, who am I to complain about being an orphan. I've always had the Lord's word as a light brightening my way." She paused. "This is the way I see things, if I came through the past with the help of the Lord, I'll do the same in the future. Anyway, the past is gone, and the future isn't here." She giggled. "It's today that I deal with, for the problems of each day is plenty to deal with. Pastor Mitchell always taught that what had to be dealt with each day was enough; there's no need trying to bring more upon ourselves than we can handle."

Anna shook her head. "I believe that's the way the Lord wants us to look at things." She paused and glanced at the box on the counter. "I think that lately I've allowed circumstances and grief to cloud my vision. I've hindered God's word from lighting my path. I've been looking at the problems of yesterday and tomorrow, when I should have just dealt with the problems of today that are enough."

Katie took a sip of coffee. "I'm a sensible person; I don't have time for negativity. Pessimism is for quitters, those who don't trust God. If faith is alive in you, you can overcome anything." She giggled. "I think I was born fighting. I remember being told that when I was dropped off at the orphanage that they thought I was too small to survive."

Anna put her right hand on Katie's left hand. "Katie Mathers! I think that I feel regenerated, something I've not felt for a while." She threw up her hands. "I do believe the Lord has sent you to me to wake me out of my spiritual slumber. You have been His means of giving me a faith booster shot. I have grieved for about four months for the girl who used to live in your house." Her heart sang with delight as she placed her hands on her hips. "But you are right, only those who don't trust God would spend time grieving for what they cannot change. We have enough problems to deal with each day that are enough. Why do we add more on top of them? No wonder, we get so weighed down with sadness." She gestured with her right hand. "I almost stopped living because of grief from losing my husband and Joan moving. After all, if Joan wanted to keep in touch, she would have done so before now."

"Maybe when you're up to it, you can tell me about her?" She picked up her coffee cup. "In the meantime, our coffee's getting cold. I hate cold coffee."

"Me too. I could never understand people who can drink cold coffee unless it's iced coffee." Anna spotted the clock. "Oh my, Katie, Pastor Matthew Beaumont will be here for lunch. He wants me to help with cooking for the church supper on Friday night." She laughed. "I don't think that we have anything to talk about, but he loves my fried chicken and potato salad." She paused. "If Byron's out of town, why don't you help me with lunch and then you can meet Pastor Beaumont. He really is a man of God. I think that you may find him to be as helpful as your Pastor Mitchell." She laughed. "It seems that I have listened to his sermons lately without actually applying their truth. Thank God that I see truth once again."

Katie's jeweled eyes sparkled. "I would love to meet him in person. Of course, I've seen him in church, but haven't actually met him. Byron likes to get out of church as soon as service is over so that he can catch up with his paperwork." She twirled a curl around her left forefinger. "I've not found any Pastor like my childhood Pastor. It would be wonderful to find one who is sincere in what the Bible teaches. I've gotten the feeling from some that they do it like a job for the money and not a calling from the Lord. Jesus warned about the hireling that doesn't care about the sheep. It's sad that so many Pastors seem like that." Katie paused. "Come to think of it, I haven't picked up that feeling from Pastor Beaumont." She giggled. "Enough of that train of thought. I'm sounding too negative. If I read my Bible, live according to its principles, go to church regularly, and pay my tithe, that's all that matters. What someone does or doesn't do is between them and the Lord. All hirelings will have to answer to God and not me."

"Amen!" Anna took a sip of coffee. "Does Byron share your beliefs?"

"I believe that he does. He said that he's a Christian and asked the Lord to save him when he was fifteen. We met in the church in my hometown. I worked at the library and he came every day. We only knew each other about two weeks when he asked me to marry him. When I saw Isaac and Rebekah in my mind, I accepted." She put her hair behind her ears with her fingers. "Anyway, he attends service with me when he's home and has no problem with me talking about the Bible. Sometimes, he's mentioned what the Pastor taught and asks me what I thought of it. We've had some really good discussions." Katie paused. "He's really so sweet. It bothers him that he will have to leave me so much, but he has no choice. His job requires a lot of travel time. Besides, you said the Lord sent me to you, but I feel He wanted us to be friends. I think that you were here for me."

Anna threw up her hands. "I do believe that we're good for each other. Right now, we better get going with Pastor Beaumont's potato salad and fried chicken."

Anna and Katie busied themselves with getting lunch while their spirits were knit together in like-minded faith. Anna finished setting the table and sat down in a chair. "Well, Katie, I do believe that this has been the best day I've had for some time." She was interrupted by the doorbell. "Goodness me, that must be the pastor." Anna got up from her seat, and they both took off their aprons. Katie hung up the aprons while Anna answered the door. "Pastor Beaumont, do come in. I have someone for you to meet. You've probably seen her at church, but now you can formally meet her."

Anna led him to the kitchen. Before she could say anything, Katie put out her left hand. "I'm Katie Mathers. Sorry that we've not properly met before, but my husband has so much business to do that he likes to get right home after church on Sunday."

Pastor Beaumont took her hand. "Well, young lady, it's a pleasure to make your official acquaintance." He reached into his pocket and handed a piece of paper to Anna. "This is the dishes that I would like you to make for Friday night." He paused as she read. "Is it acceptable to you?"

Anna displayed a wide grin. "This is fine." She gestured with her right hand toward Katie. "It seems that I'll have some help with this. Her husband is away on a business trip, and she's more than eager to help me."

Katie giggled. "She already knows me, and it has only been about a month that I've been her neighbor."

Anna motioned toward the table. "Let's take a seat and eat our lunch. I'll get the potato salad out of the refrigerator while Katie gets the fried chicken on the table." She paused. "Do you want iced tea or lemonade?"

Pastor Beaumont stroked his jaw with his left hand. "Um, I think that I'll have iced tea with this, lemonade might not go to well with potato salad."

Katie's jaw fell open. "Wow! That's exactly what Pastor Mitchell said about lemonade and potato salad when I was a child." She gestured toward Anna. "She said that you might turn out to be like my childhood Pastor from the orphanage." She put her hair behind her ears with her fingers. "I think that the Lord is going to do something wonderful here. I can't explain it, but it's like the Holy Spirit is impressing upon my heart that the two of you are now an essential part of my life."

Pastor Beaumont rubbed his hands together. "Well, Katie Mathers, as you were saying that, I felt the Lord confirm your words. I have no idea what this is all about, but there is something going on that involves the three of us." He paused. "God will make it all clear in His time." He gazed at the fried chicken. "But for now, I surely would like some of that fried chicken."

Katie giggled. "Anna said that you really enjoy her fried chicken. From the looks of it, I can't wait to have some myself."

Anna filled the Pastor's plate with chicken and potato salad. "Pastor, would you give the blessing? I think we've done enough talking, for I suddenly feel quite famished."

They all bowed their heads as the pastor gave thanks. "Lord, we thank you for this food and ask that you bless it to our bodies. In Jesus Name, Amen."

"Amen!" Anna and Katie said in unison.

Katie bit into her chicken and mumbled through a mouthful. "I've never tasted anything like this. It's better than the chicken places." She swallowed and took a drink of iced tea. "Anna, I was thinking that if you don't mind, whenever Byron is away, we could make Monday's our fried chicken and potato salad day." She giggled. "We could invite Pastor Beaumont to join us."

Before Anna could respond, the pastor nodded. "That's sounds like a great idea to me."

Anna laughed. "Well, I guess the two of you have made up my mind for me."

3

THE LOVE OF A MOTHER

The next year found Anna ignoring the portents she felt about Katie's house. After all, it had been the means that brought her Katie, the daughter she'd always desired. She found herself loving Katie more dearly than she had ever loved anyone besides Daryl. Katie was always so thoughtful and considerate. Anna found herself thanking the Lord daily for her. They went to church together, shopped, took long walks, made quilts, or played bridge; and whenever Byron was away, Katie stayed with Anna. Of course, Monday was their fried chicken and potato salad day with Pastor Beaumont as their guest, who became a great help with their quilt making.

This particular night Anna and Katie were each sitting on an end of the cabriole-leg sofa watching *Chariots of Fire*. Katie had just purchased the DVD. They had a freshly made batch of popcorn set on a maple oval-top trestle coffee table with key toned center rail and turned spindle supports. On each side of the sofa was a bookcase-lamp table where they each sat their glass of iced tea on coasters. They were about thirty minutes into the movie, when Katie reached to pick up the remote from the coffee table and paused the film. "Anna," she said, "I don't mean to pry, but I was wondering if Joan was like a daughter?"

"I truly love Joan, but she seemed more like a younger sister. I never had any siblings, and her age would have fit a younger sister."

She gestured with her hands. "We were like sisters. She was several years older than you, and I never thought of her as a daughter." She reached over and patted Katie's hand. "You, my dear, are the first to fill that depiction for me."

Katie's jeweled eyes teared. "I never thought that I'd experience the love of a mother. It sure touches the emotions. Sometimes, I feel that I married Byron, so that I could meet you." She giggled. "After all, if I hadn't married him, I would not have met you. Just to think of never knowing you makes me want to cry. I truly feel as though you have been my mother all my life. My spirit always knew that there was someone to fill that desire of my heart. I just had to wait until it was God's timing."

"I more than understand about a mother and daughter love. God is truly good." Anna gestured with her right hand. "Only God can make a heart so glad. I also know what you mean about feeling as though it has always been. That's how God does things. When the Lord is in on something, it just fits into place." She sighed heavily and felt her nerves tense. Why did Joan's name retrieve the foreboding about that house? Was she missing something under her nose?

Katie placed her hair behind her ears with her fingers. "I guess it's a good thing, because you'll be seeing a lot more of me." Her jeweled eyes sparkled. "It seems that I'll practically be living here."

Anna's eyebrows scrunched. "What do you mean?"

"Because of a big promotion, Byron told me last night that he'll be overseas much of the next few years. He'll be gone for months and months at a time." She giggled. "He said that I can take you anywhere that I want. I'm not to be concerned about spending money; he wants me to be happy. He was disappointed that I don't spend much money."

Anna's throat constricted with fear. "W-will you be moving?"

"Of course not! Byron knows how close I've become to you. He understands that I never had a mother."

"I've never understood how these businessmen can leave their wives so much." Anna said with frustration rising in her voice. "I just thank God that Daryl believed that a wife and husband should be best friends and do things together."

"I don't mind that he'll be gone so much," Katie giggled. "I get to spend more time with you. Anyway, I didn't marry Byron out of love. Remember that I told you that I married him because when he asked me, I saw Isaac and Rebekah in my mind. So I figured that was the Lord showing me that there was no way Isaac and Rebekah were in love before she became his wife." She twirled a curl around her left forefinger. "I'm not sorry that I married him, he is truly wonderful to me. To be honest, I'm quite content. Although he's away a lot, I have you. Besides, before he left last night, Byron promised a European tour before the five years."

"What does five years mean?"

"Before we were married, Byron expected this promotion and knew he'd be away often. He felt bad and promised something special to celebrate our fifth wedding anniversary."

"You're sure a promotion doesn't mean a move?"

"He swore we'd stay unless there's an offer that he can't refuse."

"That's what they all say. They claim that they must move because their husband received an offer too good to refuse. It meant an incredible pay raise and a promotion where he won't have to travel anymore. However, it meant moving far away from Hunts Grove."

Katie cupped Anna's hand. "Don't fret. I've told him I won't move without you. I don't think that he realized how stubborn I can be if I believe that God doesn't want me to do something." She giggled. "He knows that I won't do anything that I sense the Holy Spirit pricking my heart not to do. I'll admit that he was taken aback the first time that I was going to go shopping and I felt not to go." She put her hair behind her ears with her fingers. "He asked me why I believed that I shouldn't go, and I told him that the Lord was impressing that I shouldn't go today." She gestured with her hands. "So, you see, he knows that I won't move if I believe that the Lord doesn't want me to."

Anna gave a slow smile.

Katie jumped up. "Anna! You know what?"

Anna held her heart with both hands. "Besides your practically scaring me half to death, I have no clue."

"Byron will be gone about six months overseas this time. He felt ghastly about the length of time, but he again confirmed that we would take a European tour before the five years end."

Anna's eyebrows scrunched together. "I know that you said that he knew about a promotion that would keep him away often and promised the trip to celebrate your fifth anniversary. But why does he keep saying before the five years end? What does he mean about the five years ending?"

"I told you before we were married, he said that he'd be away often but promised that we'd do something extra special before our fifth wedding anniversary to make up for all the time that he'd have to be gone. It's just that he doesn't want our fifth anniversary to come and we've not done anything special." Katie's jeweled eyes sparkled. "But I think you and I can take advantage of this time that he'll be away. After all, Byron told me to take you anywhere that I want and to spend whatever I desire."

Anna's eyebrows scrunched together. "What do you mean?"

"I know that it's about two years since Joan moved, but I was thinking. What if we go to Atlanta for a few weeks? The expense is on me. Byron told me that he doesn't make the money for it to sit in the bank. He wants me to enjoy myself. What do you think? We could look up Joan." Katie gestured with her hands. "After all, I would really like to meet her from all you've told me about her."

Anna's eyes beamed. "When do you want to leave?"

"As soon as we can pack and make the flight arrangements."

Anna fidgeted with her wedding ring. "We better let Pastor Beaumont know. He'll truly miss his Monday fried chicken."

Katie giggled. "Well, we'll just have to make him double the next time, so he can take some home." She paused and twirled a curl around her left forefinger. "It's strange that he's not married; he has to be in his late thirties." She giggled. "When I first saw him in church, I thought that he looks like some Jane Austen protagonist with ash blond hair and blue eyes. He reminds me of a Darcy without the stiff personality. He's much friendlier and doesn't seem to think that he's superior to others." She gestured with her right hand. "I guess that's his business whether he's married or not. He is truly a genuine man of God. He actually lives the Bible that he preaches."

Anna reached into the popcorn bowl and sat back. "He told me that he's not married because God told him to stay single like the Apostle Paul for a while and that when he marries, he will be like Amos." She gestured with her right hand. "He understands the apostle but not the prophet. Anyway, he believes that God is keeping him single until the wife that He has for him is ready to marry him." She gave out a heavy sigh. "What an incredible man of God he is. All he wants is to do whatever God wants him to do."

§

Pastor Beaumont had insisted that he drive them to the airport and pick them up when they return from Atlanta. He retrieved their suitcases from his trunk. "Anna, I believe this one is yours, and Katie, this one must be yours."

Katie's jeweled eyes smiled. "Pastor, this one is Anna's and that one is mine."

He stroked his jaw with his left hand. "Well, at least I have you both at the right airport." The pastor looked at his watch. "Oh my, I have an appointment with Mr. Olsen in forty-five minutes." He hurried to get back in the car and turned to face them. "The Lord watch over you both and bring you back safe." Opening his car door, he paused. "Make sure you let me know when you are returning, I don't want you two waiting for me."

They all laughed, Anna and Katie picked up their suitcases, and headed for the entrance. Katie giggled as they walked up to the automated glass doors into the airport. "Well, we're finally ready to go to Atlanta." She followed Anna through the doors and perused the long open area leading to multiple airline check-in counters with luggage scales. She whispered to Anna. "I don't believe that we'll have any problem with weights with these small suitcases. After all, how much is needed for a couple of weeks?" She gestured with her left hand. "I'm sure glad that you had some experience in how to pack a suitcase for a trip. I had no idea how to pack or what to take. If it had been left up to me, I probably would have had all kinds of suitcases." She giggled. "I'm amazed that we have all that we need in these suitcases. Plus, we have a small iron to take care of any wrinkles."

Anna laughed. "Well, my experience is about twenty years old, but I believe that we have all we need. Besides, if we need anything, we can always pick it up in Atlanta like you said." She gestured to her left. "Well, there's our airline. I guess that we better get in line."

Katie gestured to her right. "If for some reason our flight is delayed, we can sit in that restaurant and have a coffee."

"I think that I would rather have something cold. I've never really been a coffee drinker after breakfast. Tea has always been my favorite. I started drinking coffee in the morning because of Daryl, but it has never been agreeable to me." She laughed. "I guess I would fit in just fine in England among the tea drinkers."

Katie gave out a heavy sigh. "My goodness! Anna, why didn't you tell me that before? I really don't enjoy coffee either, but I thought other people do. All this time, we both could have been enjoying our tea." She giggled. "I especially love loose leaf Chinese tea. As a matter of fact, I have plenty at home. When I'm alone, that is what I drink. Now, we both can have it when we get back from Atlanta. And in the meantime, we will have tea at breakfast and whenever."

Anna's belly shook with laughter. "It looks like the Atlanta trip has already had a positive outcome. My grandmother and I always had Chinese loose-leaf tea." She paused. "The silver tea set on my hutch is what she used. It seems that tea tastes so much richer in a silver tea pot. The first cup of tea that we have when we get back will be some of your Chinese loose-leaf tea in my silver tea pot."

They both got in their line, while Katie took care of every-thing. "This is the first time that I've really relished spending money. I can't explain my elation, but it's because I feel that it's what you needed."

Anna took Katie's right hand. "I think that I feel happy because we're doing this together."

Katie giggled. This will be my first time on an airplane. We were going to go overseas on our honeymoon, but at the last-minute Byron had to cancel because of someone at work having a terrible accident. He had to take the man's place. I told him it didn't matter to me. Besides, he told me that he had purchased a house for us." Her jeweled eyes sparkled. "The excitement of having my own home was like a honeymoon. However, I never expected the Lord to not only bless me with a beautiful home, but you are the best blessing that I have ever had. I thank Him daily for bringing you into my life."

Anna gave her a hug. "My dear, you are replicating my daily prayer, but mine is thanking Him for you. My life has been filled with happiness since the Lord brought you into my life." She placed her hands on her hips. "Besides, it was you that He sent to get me out of my lethargy. Grief can have a negative effect on one's faith. I don't know how I let it overtake me, but I thank God that it is gone. Yes, I miss Daryl and probably always will, but grief gone unchecked can be unhealthy. I believe what triggered the depressing response was when Joan didn't keep in touch. I then let loneliness pile on top of my grief until I saw no way out." She grabbed Katie's right hand and cupped it in hers. "That's why I can't thank God enough for sending you into my life. He's so awesome."

Katie gestured toward the flight information display system. "It seems that our flight is going to be an hour late because of some kind of delay." She giggled. "I think that it's time for us to have a cup of tea. If they have any pie, I love a piece of pie with a cup of tea."

Anna clasped her hands together. "Katie Mathers, you definitely sound more like a daughter each day. My grandmother and I used to love to have a cup of tea and a piece of pie after she just baked a fresh one."

Katie's jeweled eyes sparkled. "I believe that perhaps it is you who are sounding more like a mother each day."

They both laughed and headed for the restaurant.   19

4

NOT AN ANGEL

Atlanta proved to be much more of a metropolitan than Anna realized. At least Katie had booked them into a hotel, so the taxi driver took them there. Anna sat at the edge of her bed and perused their suite. It was set up with a kitchen containing food and drinks. She was amazed at how modern rooms had become since she last stayed in one about twenty years ago. "Katie, how will we ever find Joan in this city? I have no clue as to where to start. This place is so huge, and I have no idea if they live in the city or the suburbs. How will we ever find them?"

Katie's jeweled eyes sparkled as she held up a telephone book. "Right here. I mean, after all, how many George Tyler's can there be in the vicinity? Even if they moved, we could probably get a forwarding address."

Anna shook her head. "They never left one in Hunts Grove. I tried to get one from the Post Office. All their mail kept building up in their mailbox, until the Post Office realized that the house was vacant and stopped delivering."

Katie put her hair behind her ears. "Um, that is strange." She picked up the telephone book. "Well, right now, let's start here." She turned the pages and fingered down the list of names. "Anna! I found a G. Tyler. I'll dial the number for you."

Anna's hands were trembling when Katie handed her the phone. She listened to it ring and heard a male voice on the answering machine. "I'm sorry, but I'm unable to take your call at present. Please leave your name and number at the tone, and I'll get back with you as soon as possible." Anna gently placed the receiver down and fidgeted with her wedding ring.

Katie touched Anna's right shoulder. "Is something wrong? Are you okay?"

"It was an answering machine. I had no idea what to say, so I hung up."

Katie twirled a curl around her left forefinger. "No problem. We'll just take a taxi to the address and give Joan a surprise visit."

Anna felt her stomach fluttering all the way to the Tyler residence.

Katie spoke to the driver. "Could you please wait for us? We're not sure if we have the correct Tyler." She giggled. "If we don't, we have no idea where we are or how we'll get another taxi back to the hotel."

They both walked up the steps to the front door and Anna rang the doorbell. When the door opened, Anna stepped back. "Please forgive us for being here, but we were looking for a George and Joan Tyler. You wouldn't happen to know them or where they live?"

Mrs. Tyler shook her head. "I'm sorry, but this is the address of Graham Tyler." She sighed. "The only George Tyler that I know is married to a Margaret."

Anna fidgeted with her wedding ring. "Do you happen to know his age?"

"Yes, I do. We attended his wedding last Saturday. He is twenty-two."

"We're sorry to bother you, but the George that I'm looking for is in his late fifties. Please forgive the inconvenience that we may have caused you." Anna put her right hand out. "Thank you for your time. I hope you have a lovely evening."

"There's no inconvenience. You have a pleasant evening, and I hope you find who you're looking for."

Anna and Katie were quite melancholy when they got back into the taxi. Katie spoke to the driver. "Could you bring us back to the hotel? For your patience, I will give you a hundred-dollar tip."

When he dropped them off, he thanked Katie profusely. "I can't thank you enough. This is an answer to prayer. I had been sick and missed some days of work, and I was going to be a hundred dollars short for my rent. Wait until I tell my wife."

Katie reached into her purse and pulled out some bills and handed them to the driver. "The Lord impressed upon me that your car needs some work."

The driver had to keep back tears. "This is five hundred dollars. That's what the mechanic said it would cost to have the repairs." He grabbed Katie's right hand. "Are you sure you're not an angel sent from God?"

Katie giggled. "God sent me, but I'm not an angel. I'm just as human as you." She paused and reached into her pocketbook. "Here is another five hundred dollars for those things that have been needed, but finances have prohibited it."

"The Lord bless you abundantly for your giving heart." He shook his head. "I've heard testimonies of things like this, but I am overwhelmed that it happened to me. I can't wait to give this testimony in church tomorrow morning." He laughed. "My wife will be overcome with the joy of the Lord when I tell her what happened. She'll probably be awake all night thanking Him."

They watched him drive away, turned to go in the hotel, and took the elevator up to their suite. Once in the room, they decided to check every Tyler in the area. Not a one knew a George Tyler in his fifties.

Anna rubbed the back of her neck with her right hand. "This is so bizarre. I know Joan said they were moving to Atlanta. Besides, I helped her the day she was moving and I saw the moving slip say Atlanta."

Katie dropped the telephone book. "Do you remember the name?"

"Yes, it was Do Right Moving Company."

"That's it!" She looked at her watch. "It's after five o'clock, so they're probably closed. But first thing in the morning, I'll call the moving company and see where they delivered the belongings." She paused and gazed at the kitchen. "I'm quite hungry, but I don't think anything in there will be sufficient. Perhaps, we should go to the restaurant across the street. I think it's a Chinese Buffet." She giggled. "I love Chinese food as much as I love their loose-leaf tea. Besides, I think that an all I can eat is what I need at present."

Anna held her stomach. "My rumbling stomach quite agrees."

§

First thing the next morning after showering and enjoying their tea with cinnamon buns, Katie called information and obtained the number of the moving company. After being on the phone for about thirty minutes, she was told that they moved everything into Handy Storage in Atlanta. When she called the storage place, they said that after ninety days of the owner not paying the storage, everything was auctioned off.

Anna sat back in her chair. "It's as if they vanished from the face of the earth. This is all so incredible."

Katie hung her head. "I feel so wretched for bringing you here. Can you forgive me?"

Anna stood up and cupped Katie's face in her hands. "Forgive you for trying to make me happy? I believe that you and Joan would have taken to each other. Joan was somewhat of an introvert, but you would have brought her out of it."

"If she loved you, we'd have to take to each other." Katie gazed at Anna with tears streaming down her face. "You're the only person that has ever felt like a mother to me. The orphanage had some godly woman, but they always felt like an aunt or something. The connection in the heart was never there."

Anna kissed Katie's forehead. "I know what you are talking about. I've had some good friends, like Joan, but never the heart connection of a mother and daughter." She wiped her eyes. "Well, Katie, my dear, God doesn't want us down about things that we cannot change." She placed her hands on her hips. "I thought we came on vacation. Let's start today by visiting the High Museum of Art. There seems to be so many museums here." Anna sat back and folded her arms. "I'm really excited to be able to do this. It's been years, since I've had a vacation." She laughed and gestured with her hands. "My last vacation was my honeymoon. Daryl had to work so much that he needed his vacation to catch up on things around the house. But the Bible says that if we delight ourselves in the Lord, that He will give us the desires of our heart." She rubbed the back of her neck with her right hand. "First, He gives me the daughter of my dreams, and then He gives me the vacation that I have wanted for years."

Katie gave Anna a hug. "Well, today is the perfect time to start enjoying our vacation." She giggled. "All we have to do is call a taxi and have the driver take us to the Museum. That sure does make things easier than trying to find the places ourselves. Our driver will be our personal chauffeur."

Anna laughed. "Daryl was terrible for finding places. He said that's why God made me his navigator. I just seem to be blessed with an incredible sense of direction. However, riding in a taxi is like having a chauffeur."

Katie giggled. "Wouldn't it be something to ride in a vehicle with a real chauffeur? I always used to think of things like that when I was a young girl reading my Jane Austen novels. However, the Lord keeps me from going off into the clouds. I don't mind being who He created me to be. I'm just so blessed." She gestured with her hands. "God is so awesome!"

"Amen, to that. He has always helped me through so much I never knew my father; he died in an accident when I was only eight months old. My mother died in a boating accident when I was about six." She paused. "Come to think of it, if it wasn't for my grandmother, I would have been an orphan. There was no other family, as both my parents were an only child. Besides, my father's parents died before I was born, and my mother's father died when she was sixteen."

"Wow! You were only a grandmother away from being an orphan like me."

"Yes, but I thank God for my grandmother. She was a very godly woman and taught me so many things about faith." She fidgeted with her wedding band. "Grandmother would not have been pleased with my lethargy after Daryl died and Joan moving away." Anna held Katie's right hand. "But she would sure have taken to you. I know that she would have loved a great granddaughter full of faith in the Lord."

§

Pastor Beaumont was beside himself waiting for Anna and Katie to return from Atlanta. He folded his hands. "I don't want to call them and frighten them." He paused and looked up. "Oh Lord, please protect Katie. That dream last night has me all alarmed, but I feel strongly that it's the future and not the present." He was interrupted by the phone ringing. "Hello, this is Pastor Beaumont, may I help you?"

Katie giggled. "Yes, you can come and pick us up at the airport. We didn't call you earlier, because we didn't want to wake you so early in the morning. We caught the five-thirty flight and knew you'd be in bed. It was a last-minute decision on our part. It seems that we both felt the Lord wanted us back as soon as possible. I can't explain it, but we were to get back quickly."

The pastor shot his left fists in the air. "Praise the Lord, you have no idea. I'm on my way. I really must talk to you."

Katie hung up the phone. "That's strange. Pastor Beaumont says that he must really talk to me. He sounded anxious." She gave a heavy sigh. "I do hope nothing has happened to Byron."

Anna placed her right hand on Katie's left shoulder. "I don't believe that it's anything like that. It's a foreboding sense, but it's not Byron's death. I just think that we should remain calm until Pastor Beaumont can tell us what it is."

Katie put her hair behind her ears with her fingers. "Yes, listen to me being fearful and not having faith. How quickly we can yield to fear." She paused. "Besides, if something had happened, what can I do? Only as I trust in the Lord can I get through anything. It's Him that has helped me to overcome many obstacles in my life. Fear will only cause the obstacles to overcome me."

"That's the way I see it. I know I let grief sway me into a lethargic state of mind for a while, but He sent you to me to get me back on course." Anna scratched the back of her head with her right hand. "It is strange how we can let grief, fear, or other emotions get the better of us. Thank God that He doesn't give up on us and his Holy Spirit is always prompting us in the right direction."

Katie looked at the automated glass doors. "Oh my, Pastor Beaumont is already here. That was quick. He must really want to talk to me."

Pastor Beaumont took both of their suitcases. "I called a taxi, so I could get here fast." He gestured to the front of the airport. "That Ready Taxi is ours. I know that I won't be able to talk until we get to Anna's, but I felt the need to get here quickly. So, you can tell me about your trip on the way."

They all got seated in the taxi and Pastor Beaumont told the driver where to take them. He then gestured to Anna and Katie. "Let's hear about your trip. Was it successful?"

Anna fidgeted with her wedding band. "There was not a trace of them ever being in Atlanta. Furthermore, anyone with the last name of Tyler didn't have any relatives named George who was in his fifties."

Katie leaned forward. "To top it off, they did have all their belongings placed into storage in Atlanta." She lowered her voice. "But the strange thing is that they never paid the storage company and all their belongings were auctioned off. I mean, who just let's all their belongings go?" She gestured toward Anna. "Anna said that she knows that all they both had was a small suitcase for their trip. Everything was in the moving van."

The pastor stroked his jaw with his left hand. "That does sound quite bizarre. It's something from a mystery novel."

Anna scratched the back of her head with her right hand. "I know what you mean. It's like they vanished off the face of the earth without a trace."

"But I'm sure the Lord will bring to light anything that may be hid in darkness." The pastor laughed. "Now you both know the title of this week's sermon. The Lord has been impressing on my spirit that the devil has been trying to hide things in darkness, but the Lord is going to start shining light on hidden secrets." He scratched the back of his head with his left hand. "I believe that it's a word of wisdom from the Lord of what He is about to do."

Katie's emerald green eyes sparkled. "Wow! I know that this may seem strange, but I believe that the Lord told me a few months ago that He would bring to light that which is hiding in the darkness." She paused. "I remember that I was reading Psalm 112 where it says *Unto the upright there ariseth light in the darkness* and the Holy Spirit impressed upon my spirit that He was about to bring to light that which has been hidden in darkness." She gestured with her hands. "I believe that it has something to do with me, but I have no idea what it means. However, I truly know in my heart that God is going to do it."

Anna interrupted. "We're here, so we'll have to continue all this over a nice pot of tea. Katie you hurry and get some of that Chinese loose-leaf tea, while the pastor and I get in."

As Pastor Beaumont went to pay the driver, Katie stopped him. "If you don't mind, Pastor, this is my responsibility. The only reason for the taxi was to pick us up from the airport." She giggled. "Besides, paying the taxi driver has been a real blessing." She paid the driver and gave him a hundred-dollar tip." She pointed her left forefinger. "You take that tip and take your family some place special on your day off."

The driver's eyes bulged. "My kids have wanted to go roller skating, but I just haven't been able to afford it. I work all the hours that I can just to survive."

Katie looked him in the eyes. "You will take them roller skating, right?"

"Y-yes I will, I promise."

Katie giggled. "Good now you can take this to help with some very important needs." She then handed him two thousand dollars."

The driver fought back tears. "My wife has been washing our clothes by hand. We prayed for a new washing machine and trusted the Lord to somehow perform the miracle." He blew his nose. "This is going to take care of that, get much needed tires for the car, and other things that the kids need that have been put off." He paused and gazed at Katie. "Are you an angel from God sent in disguise? I know that some have entertained angels unawares."

Katie giggled. "I was sent by God, but I'm not an angel. I'm just human like you." She patted his right hand. "God is faithful!"

Anna and the pastor both responded in unison. "Amen!"

They got out of the taxi, Pastor Beaumont retrieved the suitcases, Katie ran across the street and Anna stood with her hands on her hips. "Well, we had better get inside. I'm still eager to find out what made you rush to the airport to pick us up. Let's get inside, and I'll get the water hot for Katie's Chinese loose-leaf tea."

Pastor Beaumont's eyebrows scrunched together. "That's really strange. How did you find out that I prefer tea? I've never said anything, because most people seem to prefer coffee. I didn't want to put anyone out."

Anna threw up her hands. "It seems that the Atlanta trip was worth it in many ways. Both Katie and I confessed that we prefer tea over coffee. We were just doing it for other people, but we really don't enjoy it. All this time we thought that we were pleasing other people, but the people weren't pleased." She laughed. "I wonder how many other people only drink coffee to please others?"

With a suitcase in each hand, Pastor Beaumont motioned toward the house. "Well, let's get in and have that cup of tea." He paused. "Do you still have some of that homemade strawberry jam? We could have some of that on whatever you have available."

Anna laughed. "I have plenty of jam left. It seems that my strawberries were abundant last year. I was able to put up almost twenty jars." She walked up the steps to unlock her door, and let them in. "Oh yes, I have some homemade scones in the freezer. I'll get them right out to thaw while we all get situated."

As they entered the house, Katie was right behind. "I brought all of it. After all, I don't want to keep running across the street to get the tea that I'll be drinking here."

Anna set the scones out, proceeded to get the water hot for the tea, and cleaned out the silver tea pot, creamer, and sugar holder. She got everything ready and put it on the silver tray. "Why don't we all sit in the den for our tea and scones? I really would enjoy sitting in my rocker recliner. Then you can tell us what it is that you have to talk to Katie about." She gasped. "Oh dear! If it's personal, you both can stay in the kitchen."

Katie giggled. "Even if it is personal, I'd only tell you any way. So, I think it's better if we both hear it together."

"I didn't mean that it was personal, the pastor said as he combed his ash blond hair back with his fingers. "To be honest, I don't know what it means." He gestured toward the tea and scones. "I think that we should all sit and eat some of those scones with jam. I'm quite hungry. I never had time for breakfast before you called."

Katie giggled. "I think that I can wait to hear what you have to say, but my grumbling stomach can't seem to wait."

Anna poured the tea using her silver strainer. They all added sugar and milk to their tea. Katie took a sip and giggled. "Wow! Tea does taste much richer from a silver tea pot. I've been drinking this tea for some time and it has never tasted so good."

Pastor Beaumont grinned. "I must admit this is the best cup of tea that I've had." He gestured with his hands. "Believe me, I truly enjoy tea. I find it so relaxing, whereas, the coffee makes me rather jittery."

Anna clasped her hands together. "That's exactly what coffee does to me."

Katie curled a curl around her left forefinger. "I wonder if drinking coffee makes people more nervous. I know that I can never finish one cup before I just don't feel quite right."

Pastor Beaumont gazed at her. "That's a good question." He grinned. "Well, at least we don't have to be concerned about not enjoying coffee when we are together. We can take pleasure in our tea."

Anna got up when they finished eating. "I'll just clear all this out of the way before we see what it is that Pastor Beaumont has to say that he doesn't know what it means."

When Anna sat back down, the pastor sat back in the cabriole leg wing chair and let out a heavy sigh. "It was last night. I'm still trying to figure out if it was a dream or a vision. I was so tired, so I don't know if I was sleeping or awake." He leaned forward. "Anyway, I saw this man kneeling in front of what looked like marble shrines or something. It seemed like he was praying, but it looked as if he was angry at God for something. When he got up, he looked at four shrines with glowing candles in silver holders. In front of all the candles were pictures of newlyweds, and in front of each picture was a little crystal coffin with wedding rings in them." He took a deep breath through his nose and let it out his mouth. "But before the thing faded, a fifth shrine almost appeared with a picture of Katie and Byron."

Anna felt a shiver go all through her. "Did you know any of the other people in the pictures?"

"I don't know, the candle light made the man's face and all the pictures so vague. The only one that was obvious was the last picture." He gestured towards Katie. "But I know her and Byron. Anyway, it is most troubling to say the least."

Katie fingered a curl with her left forefinger. "What do you mean by shrines?"

"I think that they were marble and held coffins." He scratched the back of his head with his left hand. "All I know is that I got the feeling that the people in the pictures were in those coffins. Somehow, I believe that the Lord wants you protected. I must admit that I was quite relieved when you called this morning to say that you were back."

Katie flopped back in her seat. "Wow! That's bizarre. But what am I to be protected from? Maybe I'm not to go anyplace with Byron. Apparently, whoever it is seems to be murdering the couple. If I'm not with Byron, he can't murder us." She paused. "But how do I not be in our house with him? This is quite baffling to say the least."

Anna fidgeted with her wedding ring. "I'm still having a hard time with Joan and George just vanishing." She let out a sigh. "The only thing that I do know is that we must trust the Lord to bring to light what this is all about." She gestured towards Katie with her right hand. "God promised you that He would bring to light what has been hidden in darkness. Perhaps this is the darkness that He will bring to light."

Pastor Beaumont stroked his jaw with his left hand. "I know this may be off the subject, but I try to keep up with world news. I think that we should always be aware of what is going on in Israel."

Anna stood and retrieved the remote from the television stand. "Well, I'll just turn it on. Daryl and I always kept up with world news. We felt the same way. As Christians, we need to know what is going on around us. Things have gotten so bad with people calling good evil and evil good that we must be aware. We could find ourselves close to the end time."

Katie and Pastor Beaumont both responded. "Amen to that."

They all sat and watched the world news, when a picture was placed on the screen with the words: *HAVE YOU SEEN THIS GIRL?* Anna dropped the remote, fell back in her chair, and the color drained from her face.

Katie ran over to her. "Anna, are you all right? What's wrong?"

Anna pointed to the screen. "That's Joan. That's her picture. She's a little younger in that picture, but that's her." She shook her head. "I don't understand, the news is saying that her name is Shirley Montgomery, but I'd know Joan anywhere."

Pastor Beaumont's eyebrows scrunched together. "I have seen that girl before. She shopped at the same grocery store as me. It seemed that she shopped every Friday morning, and we would see each other. She always smiled when I would wish her a good morning." He paused. "Wait a minute! She came to church with you several times after Daryl died. I remember seeing tears in her eyes when I had preached on God's love."

Katie twirled a curl around her left forefinger. "That's the Joan that we were trying to find in Atlanta?"

Anna turned up the sound on the television. "Katie, hand me that notepad and pencil on that side table. They want anyone that's seen her in the last seven years to call her uncle's solicitor." Anna took the pad and wrote down the number." She rubbed the back of her neck with her right hand. "This is most confusing, as Joan said that her uncle was dead." She shook her head. "But I know that's Joan. She was my neighbor for almost five years."

"What are you going to do?" Pastor Beaumont asked. "Are you going to call the number?" He gazed at the number on the screen. "That number is from England. I know because I had a fellow from England in Bible College with me."

Katie's face screwed up. "Joan's from England?"

Anna stared at the pad. "She did seem to have somewhat of an accent, but she never mentioned England. I never thought to ask anything about her uncle. It seemed that any time she mentioned him, she was overcome with sadness, so I never pushed."

Pastor Beaumont rubbed his hands together. "The Holy Spirit is impressing quite strongly that you should call immediately. Perhaps, the phone call will shed light on what happened."

When Anna put down the phone, Katie and Pastor Beaumont were both waiting to hear what it was all about. Katie gestured with her hands. "Well, what did he say?"

"The solicitor wants me to come to England and bring everything that I have of Joan's." She blew out a heavy sigh. "Joan's uncle is Lord William Hastings Radcliffe, the Earl of Cranston."

Katie's jeweled eyes sparkled. "Do you mean that Joan was an aristocrat?"

"I don't know, but he wants me to come as soon as possible. The earl will be paying all expenses." She paused and gazed at Katie. "I feel this strong sense that I'm to take you with me. I can't put my finger on what it is all about, but I know the Lord doesn't want me to leave without you."

Katie giggled. "I told you that you were stuck with me for life."

"So you did."

Katie's jeweled eyes twinkled. "I know that I've always complimented you on your dress and manner. But when we met, you reminded me of an aristocrat. A real lady. You hold yourself so regal with your straight back and height. Plus, your fancy French twist just adds to your aristocratic mannerism."

Anna gave Katie a hug. "Thank you for that compliment. I believe that I owe my mannerism and dress to my grandmother. She always used to say that to me." Her eyebrows scrunched together. "Someone else told me that. Who was it?" She gestured with her hands. "I remember. It was Joan, the day that I met her. When she saw me, she told me that I reminded her of a portrait of a Lady Joan. Apparently, since her name is really Shirley, that picture must be where the idea for her name came from."

Pastor Beaumont scratched the back of his head with his left hand. "Excuse me, but it's not only Katie that is supposed to go, but the Lord is prompting me to go. I'll just pawn some things to get enough money. I don't know what's going on, but you are not to go to England without the two of us."

Katie's jeweled eyes sparkled. "Well, this is going to be quite an adventure. When I was young, I read all of Jane Austen's novels. I used to dream of going to England." She clasped her hands together. "Now I get to go." She turned to the pastor. "Pastor Beaumont, the expense is mine. You have no idea how much money Byron gives me. Until the Atlanta trip, I hadn't really touched it." She put her hair behind her ears with her fingers and giggled. "At least this time when he gets home, he won't be able to complain that I didn't spend any money."

The pastor stroked his jaw with his left hand. "This will give our youth pastor a chance to take the reins. It seems that he will make a good pastor." He nodded his head. "This will allow him to preach while I'm gone. The head deacon's son has felt a call to work with the youth; this will be the perfect time for him to test the waters." He rubbed his hands together. "I guess it shouldn't take too long for us to be ready. I'll take care of the ministry part today,

pack my luggage, and inform the congregation at service tomorrow night. Then I have a few appointments on Thursday that must
be kept." He gestured with his hands. "I can be ready to leave on
Friday. That's if you can get the flights that soon."

Katie giggled. "I don't think that there should be any problem
since money is no object. I'll call the airline today and see what I
can do."

5

THE EARL OF CRANSTON'S CONFESSION

They made all the arrangements in a couple of days and were ready to catch their flight on Friday evening. Pastor Beaumont was quite surprised that Katie had booked their flight in first class. "I have always wanted to travel first class, but that was out of my price range." He clasped his hands together. "I can't get over how thrilled I am about this trip." He gestured his left hand toward Katie. "I must admit that I read all the Jane Austen novels when I was younger and always wanted to see England. All I've done the last couple of days is thank the Lord repeatedly for giving me such a blessing."

Anna sat back in her recliner seat. "This is definitely first class. These roomier seats are so comfortable." She picked up a menu. "We even have a menu." She paused and sighed. "Everything is quite nice."

Katie twirled a curl around her left forefinger. "I tried to get us first class for Atlanta but had to take coach. All the first class tickets were sold out both ways. I thought that was rather strange, but apparently there were a lot of conventions going on in Atlanta at the same time as our trip." Her eyebrows scrunched together. "It seemed feasible for the trip there, but I didn't think it made any sense for a five-thirty a.m. flight out of Atlanta." She giggled. "Well, anyway, we have first class now. It will be much more comfortable for this trip. Flying to Atlanta was only about an hour. This will probably be about nine hours." She turned to look at Anna. "May I please look at that menu? I suddenly seem very hungry."

Pastor Beaumont laughed. "You must be reading my mind."

"No," Anna said, "I think that you're both reading my mind. I don't know if the excitement or the confusion about this trip is making me hungry, but either way, I am famished."

As they waited for their dinner, Anna asked the pastor a question. "Pastor Beaumont do you have any living relations? I don't remember you ever mentioning any family."

He stroked his jaw with his left hand. "First of all, may I ask you both something?"

Katie and Anna both nodded in the affirmative.

"Would you stop calling me Pastor Beaumont, I have spent so much time with the two of you that you feel like family. Besides, I have always had a problem with such a formal title." He gestured with his hands. "After all, Jesus was called Jesus, the apostle Paul was called Paul, as was Peter, James, John and all the apostles. I can understand calling me Pastor Matthew, because Paul called himself Paul an apostle of Jesus Christ. In private, I would really appreciate you both calling me Matthew."

Katie put her right hand out. "Okay, Pastor Matthew, it's a deal."

He threw up his arms. "No, I said just plain Matthew."

Anna reached over and touched his right arm. "It may take a little time, but I will try to accommodate you."

"Now, let me answer your question about family. I believe that I may have a cousin on my mother's side, but none other that I know of. You see, my parents had me late in life. My mother was fifty. Both had no living parents and only my mother had a brother more than thirty years her senior. It seems that my grandmother had him at eighteen and my mother at fifty. She told me that her brother had a daughter that was about twelve when she was born, and that she believed she had a son later in life. But that was more than twenty years ago, when my mother passed away at the age of seventy." He let out a sigh. "So, I guess that you and Katie are the closest thing to a family that I have." His eyebrows scrunched together. "Why did you ask me that?"

"It's really strange, but you remind me so much of Daryl when he was young. It's like it never dawned on me until we've spent so much time together recently." She paused. "I was just wondering if you were related in some way. You see, Daryl was sixteen years older than me, but it never mattered to us. His elderly parents thought it was awful that he would marry someone so young and just stopped staying in touch with him. We were just so in love and very happy. We knew that the Lord brought us together. Age never played any part in our thinking. We were in the Lord's will and that's all that mattered." She let out a heavy sigh. "Of course, now, I'm alone and only forty-six. Daryl died at fifty-nine from a heart attack." She sat forward. "However, I would not have done anything differently."

"Do you happen to know any of your husband's relatives? I mean their names. Who knows, we could have been related."

Anna leaned back and closed her eyes. "Let me think. His mother's name was Elizabeth Rose La Fleur."

Before she could continue Matthew practically jumped out of his seat. "Did you say Elizabeth Rose La Fleur?"

"Yes."

"My mother's maiden name was La Fleur. Was his grandfather named John?"

Anna's eyebrows scrunched together. "Yes, it was."

"Praise the Lord! I believe that your husband's mother was my cousin. My mother's older brother was John La Fleur who had a daughter named Elizabeth Rose."

Katie giggled. "Wow! This means that you two really are family by marriage. Daryl and Matthew would be second cousins."

They were interrupted by their dinner being delivered to them. The flight attendant gave them their meals. "Would you like anything to drink?"

Katie answered. "I think that we would all like tea."

Anna and Pastor Beaumont both nodded in agreement.

While they were eating, Anna took out her wallet to show Matthew a picture of Daryl when they were married. "If I didn't know who it was, I would think it's me. We really do resemble each other." He paused and gave out a sigh. "I wish I'd have known that we were cousins before. That's why I was always drawn to him. He was not only physical family but a brother in the Lord."

They finished their meal and Anna sat back in her reclining seat. "I think it would be good for us to get some sleep. We have no idea what's ahead for us in England." She reached over and touched Matthew's arm. "Now that we're cousins, I have no problem calling you Matthew."

§

When they arrived at the airport, they were greeted by Lord Cranston's chauffeur. "I believe that you three must be Anna, Katie, and Pastor Beaumont. I'm Edmond, Lord Cranston's chauffeur. I will take you to him."

Anna watched as the red-haired man took her and Katie's suitcases. She was amazed that he put one under each arm and picked up one in each hand. "If you will follow me, I'm parked close by."

Pastor Matthew went to help with the suitcases, but the man refused. "Pastor, this is fine, I can take care of these. If I could, I would carry yours also."

Katie giggled as he stopped at a black limousine, put the suitcases down, opened the trunk, and put their suitcases inside. "We're going to ride in a limousine. This is like living a Jane Austen novel. All this is happening because God moved me to Hunts Grove. Isn't God awesome?"

Anna nodded. "We did say that it would be nice to ride in a vehicle with a chauffeur and not a taxi driver." She paused. "God is truly awesome!"

They all got situated in the limousine. Anna could feel her stomach doing cartwheels. "I can't believe how excited I feel. I almost feel like I did the first time my grandmother took me to the zoo. It's one thing to see all the animals in books or on television, but to see them alive was quite thrilling for a seven-year-old."

Katie giggled. "I know what you mean. It almost feels like I'm in some fantastic dream, but we're really in England and riding in a limousine."

The pastor scratched the back of head with his left hand. "I must admit that I have been thanking the Lord constantly for making all this possible." He gestured with his hands. "Plus, I really have a cousin. This has already been an incredible endeavor."

They all sat back enjoying the fact that they were riding in a limousine in England. Suddenly, Katie's head went forward, her eyes widened, and her mouth fell open as the chauffeur turned into the entrance of the estate. "Is this a fairy tale? Look at this place. It's like a palace or something."

Anna nodded. "I've only seen something this grand on television or in a book but seeing it in real life is quite fascinating." She gestured with her hands. "It definitely surpasses the zoo."

Pastor Matthew let out a heavy sigh. "Whew! This is what I would have expected Darcy's Pemberley to look like. It's magnificent."

Anna nodded. "Yes, every time that I read *Pride and Prejudice*, I used to think how I would have loved to be Eliza the first time she visited Pemberley and viewed its grandeur."

Katie giggled. "That's it. Yes, it is what Pemberley would look like." She paused and twirled a curl with her left forefinger. "I sure hope that the earl doesn't think me too common. After all, he's an earl, and I'm an orphan." She giggled. "*Emma* was the other Jane Austen novel that I used to imagine that I might be the daughter of a gentleman like Emma thought of Harriet Smith. However, Harriet never proved to be any more than a commoner."

Anna put her right hand on Katie's left hand. "You could never be too common. You brighten up every life that you touch."

Matthew nodded. "That's the truth. This trip to England has certainly brightened my life." He gestured with his hands. "Besides, it was you that started my weekly fried chicken and potato salad at Anna's. You have no idea how much I looked forward to that every week."

Edmond pulled up to the entrance, ushered them out of the limousine, retrieved their suitcases from the trunk, and placed the correct suitcases in front of each. Katie giggled. "Well, Matthew, he had more suitcases than you and remembered which one belonged to whom."

Before Matthew could respond, they were greeted by the butler. "I'm Michael, Lord Cranston's butler."

Anna responded. "I'm Anna Paquette." She gestured toward Katie and the pastor. "This is Katie Mathers and Pastor Matthew Beaumont. Lord Cranston knows that they are accompanying me."

The butler nodded. "One moment please." He then turned his attention to the footmen. "Take their luggage to their rooms." Once Anna, Katie, and Pastor Beaumont handed over their suitcases, the butler again turned his attention to them. "Would you please follow me? Lord Cranston is waiting for you."

"Certainly," Anna said, as she, Katie, and Pastor Beaumont followed.

Michael led them through some splendid rooms, up an enormous oak stairway with very dynamic moldings and decoration with carving on the balusters. At the landing he led them down a large hall lined with regal pictures. Anna wondered if they'd ever reach their destination, when he finally stopped at a door and knocked.

"Come in," said a strong male voice.

Michael entered and bowed. "My lord, your guests are here."

"Thank you, Michael. Show them in."

Michael ushered them into the room that had a fireplace with applied motifs, dentil work and molded panels. "My lord, this is Anna Paquette, Katie Mathers, and Pastor Matthew Beaumont." He then gestured towards the earl. "May I introduce William Hastings Radcliffe, the fifth Earl of Cranston."

When Anna was introduced, the earl's countenance took on a haunted look, but he immediately straightened himself up. "It's a delight to meet you. I pray that your journey was agreeable."

Although Anna was taken aback by the odd expression on Lord Cranston's face when she was introduced, she found herself quite impressed with William Hastings Radcliffe, the Earl of Cranston, a stately figure of man at six-foot, solid build with black and silver hair. She felt that his palatial manor and thousand acres served to complement its owner. "Lord Cranston, our trip was most agreeable. It was quite gracious of you to allow me to bring my friends. We thank you for your hospitality."

The earl gestured with his hands. "Please take a seat." He motioned to the Walnut Wing Armchair with gros-and petit-point polychrome needlework and cabriole legs ending in pad feet that was to the right of his. "Mrs. Paquette, would you please sit here, as I have much to ask you." Then he gestured toward a matching walnut sofa. "Pastor Beaumont and Katie, you both may sit there."

Anna sat down. "Before you ask me any questions, I have one request." She smiled. "Would you please call me Anna?"

He chuckled. "Anna, I believe that I can accommodate you." He turned his attention to his butler. "Michael, please pour our guests a cup of tea and then you may leave us."

"Yes, my lord."

Anna watched as Michael walked over to the Circular Teapoy with gadrooning decorating the base of the interior and carved scrolling feet. "What a magnificent William IV teapot."

Lord Cranston gave a puzzled gaze. "Thank you for your compliment. May I inquire how you knew what it was?"

"I've always been interested in antiques, and I have studied them for years."

Katie giggled. "Lord Cranston, Sir, she has antiques in all her rooms at home. They're quite gorgeous."

The earl stroked his jaw with his right forefinger and thumb. "Remarkable."

Michael interrupted. "Excuse me, but would you like sugar and milk in your tea?"

They all nodded in unison. "Yes, please."

The earl waited for Michael to give his guests their tea and to leave the room. "This is my private sitting room, but I wanted us to meet where Shirley and I always sat." He gestured toward Anna. "That was Shirley's chair. She sat there every day for our afternoon tea."

Katie's jeweled eyes sparkled. "Lord Cranston, Sir, I hope you don't mind me being here. I promise to be as quiet as a mouse unless you address me."

Pastor Matthew stroked his jaw with his left hand. "You see, Sir, we were with Anna when she saw the news about Joan, I mean Shirley. And the Lord made clear that we were to accompany her. We don't know why, but we are sure that the Lord will make known why."

The earl rubbed his bottom lip with his right forefinger. "Astonishing!" He shook his head and let out a heavy sigh and gestured towards Katie. "No, of course I don't mind you being here. I'm quite delighted to make your acquaintance." He gestured with his right hand. "Lord Cranston will suffice without the Sir."

Katie giggled. "Yes, Lord Cranston." She gave out a heavy sigh. "Whew! I'm glad to hear that. I didn't know what you being an earl and all would think of a commoner like me."

Lord Cranston gave a slow grin. "Now, let's get to business. My concern at present is to elucidate myself."

Anna leaned forward. "You don't owe us any explanation. We just . . ."

"Pardon me!" He interrupted, putting up his right hand. "But if you will be so kind, permit me to do what I must do. It's something that I should have done years ago."

Anna sensed turmoil in the man. "I'm sorry for interrupting." She gestured with her right hand. "Please go on."

"Excuse me," Pastor Beaumont interrupted, "but may I please pray?"

The earl gazed at the pastor and shook his head. "Yes, I believe that I could use the Lord's help to get this all out. It has been concealed for too many years."

Pastor Beaumont bowed his head. "Dear Lord, I sense turmoil in this man. Please touch him with your peace and give him the grace and comfort that he needs. In Jesus Name, I pray. Amen!"

The earl nodded and smiled. "Thank you, pastor." His eyes tightened as if he was trying to remember something, then shaking his head, he sat back, and folded his arms. "Shirley became cross with me about eight years ago regarding her birth and promised never to return, but I was convinced that she would be back." He cleared his throat as his eyes started to water. "Until two years ago, on the third of March, she'd say 'Happy birthday uncle' through the blower and hang up." He paused, rubbing his chin with his right forefinger and thumb, he gazed at Anna. "It's been about two years for you too, right?"

"Correct. That's when she and her husband moved to Atlanta. Although she promised to keep in touch, I've not heard a word from her."

"That's very strange. Shirley was conscientious about keeping her word." His face paled. "The first time she missed a call, I hired an enquire agent to track her down. Apparently, she left no trail. He could find nothing about her from the time she left here."

Anna leaned forward. "If you don't mind my asking, what did she learn about her birth that made her so upset?"

"She discovered that Lady Joan and I had allowed ourselves to drink too much wine at her coming out party and found ourselves in a forbidden interlude. We were extremely sorry and repented immediately and never allowed ourselves to be in that situation again." He stirred uneasily in his chair. "When Joan found herself with child, she took the shame upon herself to protect my reputation. You see, my wife had been in a riding accident when we were married for only two months. She became an invalid, but I would not hurt her." His midnight blue eyes took on a haunted look as he glared at a picture of Shirley on the mahogany table between the two chairs. "I let Joan not only suffer the humiliation while she lived, but allowed her to die in shame."

Katie twirled a curl around her left forefinger. "Are you trying to tell us that you are Shirley's father?"

He hung his head. "Yes. How that diary was kept hid in the attic, I'll never know." He paused rubbing his chin with his right forefinger and thumb and gazed at Anna. "What did Shirley tell you about her family?"

Anna fidgeted with her wedding band. "She told me that her mother died when she was quite young, that she never knew her father, that her Uncle Feathers raised her, and that she had no living relatives."

He sat back and folded his arms and starred at a portrait over the fireplace of a woman who reminded Anna of herself. "Joan, which was her mother's name, died about a week after giving birth to Shirley. She did know her father when she found the diary." He picked up his tea cup and took a sip. "She started calling me 'Uncle Feathers' when she was about two." He put the cup down, snickering. "She associated me with feathers, because I have a quill collection and would use them to tickle her nose." His eyes took on that haunted look. "That name became an endearment to the both of us." He gave a heavy sigh. "There you have it." He threw up his right hand. "Her uncle died when he became her father."

Anna touched his hand. "If it's any consolation, Shirley loved and adored her Uncle Feathers. She would always mention things that he did or said." Her eyebrows scrunched together. "There were times that she held back tears when speaking about him. It makes no sense that she would leave someone she loved that dearly."

Pastor Beaumont leaned forward. "May I interject something that I feel very strongly?"

Lord Cranston gazed at him. "Yes, of course." He gestured with his right hand. "Please speak whatever it is that you sense."

"Okay, as I was listening to all this, I believe the Holy Spirit was impressing upon me that something is terribly wrong." He looked at Katie. "It was as if He's saying that my dream is part of Lord Cranston's story. It's all quite alarming."

Lord Cranston leaned forward. "What dream? Was it about Shirley?"

"I don't know, but I know that it had something to do with Katie." He sat back and folded his arms. "Okay, let me tell you about it. There was a man that I never saw before kneeling before four marble shrines that housed coffins. On each shrine was a silver candlestick with a glowing candle. In front of each candle there was a picture of a newlywed couple and in front of each picture was a crystal coffin with wedding bands in them. But before it faded away, there was almost the appearing of a fifth picture with Katie and her husband." His eyebrows scrunched together. "But I believed that it's the future, but not really clear. It was most unsettling to say the least."

The earl gazed at Katie. "Did you know Shirley?"

"No, Sir, she lived in my house before she moved to Atlanta. Anna and I went to Atlanta recently and found no trace of her there." She leaned forward. "The strange thing was that all their belongings were sent to a storage place, but they never picked them up. It seems that the storage company sold them all at auction."

Anna handed the earl an album. "Well, not all her belongings were auctioned off. Shirley gave me something very personal to her before she moved. Those are the pictures that I have of her."

He flipped through the album. "My, she does look bonny. Did you take them?"

"Yes, George wasn't one for pictures." She grabbed her purse, opened it, and removed a tortoise shell box. She unclasped the box to reveal its contents. "In fact, Joan, I mean Shirley gave me this precious locket with a young man's picture in it, so George wouldn't destroy it."

His head went back, and his brows scrunched. "Destroy it! Whatever for?"

"He claimed something about bad luck." Anna paused as she sensed the foreboding. "Anyway, George found it when they were packing and threw it away. Joan waited until he was asleep, retrieved it from the trash, and hid it until the next morning when he went out. She brought it to me, asked me to hold onto it, and promised that she would send for it. But she never did." Anna handed the box to the earl. "I've kept it in that box ever since."

He opened the box and took out its contents. "Dear me!" His eyes took on a haunted look. "It must have been with the diary."

"You gave it to her? Is that a picture of you?"

"No, I never gave it to Shirley." He nodded his head. "Yes, it's me many years ago." He gave a heavy sigh. "You see, although Joan and I had no further relationship after that once, I promised to marry her when my invalid wife died. This locket represented my pledge."

Anna knew too well the reality of grief and fidgeted with her wedding band. "I'm sorry, it seems that I'm making things more difficult for you."

"Rubbish!" the earl said, as he placed the locket back in the box and set the box on the table. "You've not only returned my precious locket, but you've given me pictures of Shirley."

Anna couldn't help but admire this man. "I thank God that I've kept them." Anna touched his right arm. "But really, you don't have to continue your story. It's obviously very painful. After all, does it matter if we know?"

"Thank you all the same, but I want to finally make a full confession to someone besides God. First, I was attracted to Joan when she came to live with us after her parents were killed in an accident. I was only a few years older than she, but I kept my feelings to myself until that dreadful party. When she found herself with child, I made that pledge. She died in shame without naming the father to shield my good name." He cleared his throat. "My wife lived fifteen years after Joan's death, and with the passing of so much time, I didn't have the courage to tell Shirley." He threw up his right hand. "It's always the same excuse of honor or some blooming reason."

Pastor Beaumont stroked his jaw with his left hand. "Lord Cranston, did you do it out of love for your wife?"

"Yes, I did. It was difficult with an invalid wife. But outside of that one time, I remained faithful to my marriage vows." He cleared his throat. "Matilda, my wife, suffered so with her condition. I couldn't hurt her, and Joan thought of her as a sister." He took on a haunted look. "But there was no reason for my not owning that Shirley was my daughter after Matilda died."

"I know that all this is difficult," Pastor Beaumont said, "but you have to accept that God has forgiven you. Guilt and condemnation is not of God. You must understand that when you have repented, God forgives, and it is forgotten. Isaiah chapter forty-three verse twenty-five makes clear that for his own sake, God does not remember the sins that are forgiven. It is the devil that torments you with this. Besides, Shirley knows that you are her father, and that's all that really matters."

Lord Cranston rubbed his bottom lip with his right forefinger. "I don't know what has just happened, but I feel such a release. Maybe that's why you had to come with Anna. It never occurred to me that Shirley knows who I am, and that is all that matters. All this guilt has had me in its grip, when God has forgiven me." He gave out a heavy sigh. "The anguish is gone at last."

Pastor Beaumont nodded his head. "Exactly, but I still think that something must be done to find her."

Katie twirled a curl around her left forefinger. "I believe you're right. It's like I'm getting this strong impression from the Holy Spirit that Shirley's disappearance does have something to do with your dream about me."

Lord Cranston rubbed his chin with his right forefinger and thumb. "All of this mystery seems like an *Agatha Christie* novel. I've always enjoyed her Hercule Poirot and Miss Marple mysteries, but reading a mystery and living one is totally different. I never contemplated that I might be in the middle of one. All this is rather peculiar."

Anna fidgeted with her wedding band. "I know what you mean. My late husband said that I read too many *Agatha Christie* mysteries. It seems that I have had a foreboding about Katie's house for many years, but Daryl attributed it to my reading too many Miss Marple mysteries."

The earl's eyebrows scrunched together. "What do you mean a foreboding?"

"Her house sells about every five and a half years or so. It seems like all the couples are newlyweds that move in, the husband gets a promotion too big to refuse, and they move about a couple of months or so before five years. Five couples have lived in that house since I first moved into the neighborhood." She rubbed the back of her neck with her right hand. "It just doesn't seem natural. How come each husband that moves into that house is a traveling businessman who is away from home often? I have tried to find a connection, but I come up blank."

Katie's jaw dropped. "Wow! I didn't know that many people have lived in my house. All I knew about was Joan, I mean, Shirley. This is beginning to sound like a scary mystery."

Pastor Beaumont scratched the back of his head with his left hand. "I'm not trying to add drama to this mystery, but the Lord is strongly impressing that we must find Shirley as soon as possible." He gestured toward the earl. "I know that you said that you hired someone to find her and came up empty. We also know that Anna and Katie went to Atlanta and what they found is most troubling. Who would have all their belongings put into storage and never pay the storage? It's all becoming more and more bizarre. Especially that we now know that she is the daughter of an earl. Too many things are not adding up."

Lord Cranston rubbed his chin with his right forefinger and thumb. "I think that it would be wise to call in Scotland Yard. Perhaps, I should have had my friend Inspector Philip Gauthier in on this before. But I believed that Shirley would come home." He took on a haunted look. "Now, I don't know what to think. It is so out of character for her to ignore my birthday. She always felt that was my special day and she enjoyed making it unique. I have this dreadful sense that I will not see her again."

Anna patted his right hand. "Never give up hope that all this will come out somehow for the good. I don't understand what that means, but I believe that the Lord is doing something good. We must trust Him."

Katie twirled a curl around her left forefinger. "That's the one thing that I've always known. I was raised in an orphanage and never knew my parents. However, when you have no one, the Lord has a way of making Himself known. I had a pastor that taught me that I had the best father of all. God was my Father and He loved me more than any parent could. The Lord has always been a light brightening my life." She flushed. "I don't mean to rattle on, but I just know that the Lord is doing something positive."

Lord Cranston smiled. "You are not rattling. I think that I needed a faith booster. It seems that I have let myself become quite discouraged for some time. When that happens, I believe that we can become overwhelmed with the negative and focus on that instead of our God."

Anna threw up her hands. "It seems that Katie has been the means of giving a few of us a faith booster. When I first met her, I was grieving the loss of my husband and Shirley not keeping in touch. She just let the Lord shine through her, and I was lifted out of my lethargy." She gestured toward Katie. "It seems that Katie Mathers brightens up the life of everyone she touches."

The earl sat back and folded his arms. "Well, I think the first thing on the agenda is contacting Philip and see what Scotland Yard can do."

6

THE EARL'S SECRET GARDEN

After Inspector Philip Gauthier left, Anna stood with her hands on her hips. "Lord Cranston, have you noticed how the inspector could almost be a twin to Hercule Poirot? However, his mustache isn't quite right."

"Yes, I have joshed him about that many times. In jest, I have called him Hercule. Of course that is only in private. I respect him too much to do it publicly."

Pastor Beaumont chuckled. "To be honest, I thought that I was living in a Hercule Poirot mystery when he walked in. He is quite an impressive figure. But when he ever spoke French, it was all I could do not to call him Hercule."

The earl gestured with his right hand. "He's a good sport. As a matter of fact, he takes being thought of as Poirot as a great compliment. Once, he said to me that he would love to épater le bourgeois like Poirot and fastidiously solve all crimes." The earl noticed Katie's face screw up. "Katie is something wrong?"

Katie twirled a curl around her left forefinger. "It looks as though I'm the only one here that doesn't speak French. Pastor Beaumont seems to speak it and Anna's husband was French and taught her." She gestured with her hands. "I had no idea what the inspector said when he spoke French, and I have no idea what you just said."

"I'm sorry. It's just that my tutor was French and taught me the language. I forget that many people do not speak it." He smiled. It means that he would love to bedazzle and befuddle people like Poirot."

Katie giggled. "Listening to all of you talk about the Agatha Christie mysteries makes me want to read them. I guess I was so much into Jane Austen. I did read all of Charles Dickens and the Bronte sisters. However, I was as intrigued with Charlotte Bronte's *Jane Eyre* as I was with Jane Austen's novels. I think it was because Jane was an orphan that raised herself above all her hardship to end up marrying Mr. Rochester." She put her hair behind her ears. "There were other classics that I enjoyed, but I don't remember ever reading anything by Agatha Christie." She threw up her hands. "Now, I'm really convinced that I had better read some when we get home."

Lord Cranston motioned with his right hand. "My personal reading material is in those glassed cabinets. I have all of Agatha Christie's mysteries. Plus, you'll find Jane Austen, Charles Dickens, the Bronte sisters, Wilkie Collins, and all the classics. You are welcome to start reading Hercule Poirot or Jane Marple today." He paused. "The only requirement is that you take one book from here at a time, and put it back in its place when you are finished."

Her jeweled eyes sparkled. "Thank you, I think that I will start with Hercule Poirot. I want to see what Anna meant when she said that the inspector's mustache isn't quite right."

Pastor Beaumont chuckled. "Anna is right. The inspector's mustache just doesn't seem to be Poirot. However, he is what I would expect Poirot to be like. It's amazing to watch and to listen to him."

§

A week later found Inspector Gauthier giving the Earl the results of the Yard's efforts to track down the Tyler's. "My lord, our efforts to find the Tyler's has come up empty. We have tried every known avenue to locate them." He gestured with his hands. "It is most *déroutant*. In fact, it is as if a George and Joan Tyler their ages never existed. If we found a George Tyler, there was no Joan. If we located a Joan Tyler, there was no George. We did find a couple with the name of George and Joan Tyler, but their ages were not what we were looking for. It's as if they *disparu* from the face of the earth." He brushed something off his left shoulder with his right hand. "However, we did manage to track Shirley Montgomery leaving England and arriving in New York, but after that she just *disparu*." He gestured with his right hand. "*C'est tout.*"

Anna fidgeted with her wedding band. "If I hadn't known Joan Tyler for five years, I would believe that she never existed. None of this is making any sense." She paused. "Wait a minute!" She gestured toward the earl. "The locket that Shirley had given me might have latent fingerprints on it." She gazed at the inspector. "I'm aware that forensic science can now develop fingerprints several years old using ninhydrin. Perhaps it may have George's fingerprints on it. After all, he did handle it."

"*C'est une bonne idée.* May I please see the locket?"

Katie giggled. "Excuse me, I don't mean to interrupt. It's just quite difficult to follow what is being said when I can't speak or understand French." She paused. "What was said before he asked for the locket?"

Anna laughed. "He said that I had a good idea."

"I think that learning French needs to be something that I also have to do." She giggled. "You're all making me feel pretty ignorant."

Pastor Beaumont scratched the back of his head with his left hand. "Well, that's something that I can do. My mother was French and taught me the language before I started school. Then when I had to take a foreign language, I took French. That helped me with reading and writing the language more fluently." He gestured with his hands. "I have been teaching some of the youth in the church. It seems that the Lord revealed a way to help them learn more quickly than usual. They were flunking their French class in school. After a couple of months, they were acing the class."

Katie's jeweled eyes sparkled. "Can we start now?" Her face flushed. "I mean after the inspector leaves."

The inspector addressed the earl. "If you have the locket handy, I will be on my way. There's much I need to *acccomplir*."

Lord Cranston handed him the case with the locket. "It's in here. The less people that touch it will give the experts a better opportunity for George Tyler's fingerprints to be found." He gave out a heavy sigh. "I do pray that it helps solve this mystery. Shirley must be found."

"*Je vous remercie.*" He gave a bow with his head. "If you will excuse me, I will be on my way." He gestured toward Katie with his right hand. "You may now start your *François leçons.*"

Katie giggled. "I don't know French, but I believe that he said that I may start my French lessons."

Anna clasped her hands. "I do believe that she will turn out to be a quick study with her French lessons."

Pastor Beaumont rubbed his hands together. "Well, I had better get started teaching her, before she learns it on her own." He gazed at the earl. "Lord Cranston, may I have some paper and pencil? Is there a special room that you would recommend us doing the lessons?"

"Yes, to both questions. My butler will show you to the library that has all you will need." He gestured toward Katie. "You will also find all the books there that are in my personal collection with thousands of others. It has about anything you could look for in a library. You may sign out several books at a time." He gestured toward his glass cabinets. "This collection belonged to my mother and that's why I'm rather protective of its contents." He paused. "Pastor Beaumont, the library also contains all the books that my tutor used in teaching me French. You are welcome to use them if they will help."

The pastor stroked his jaw with his left hand. "Yes, I think that I would like to see if they would help me to teach her more quickly. This way she could study on her own. I think that she'll pick up the language rather quickly."

Katie giggled. "Now, if the inspector spoke Spanish, I would be able to help all of you. It seemed that at the orphanage, Spanish was the language of several of the workers. So, most of us learned Spanish very early."

The earl rang for his butler, who promptly entered the room. "What is it, my lord?"

Lord Cranston gestured toward the pastor and Katie. "Michael, would you please show Pastor Beaumont and Katie to the library. It seems that the pastor needs my old French books. Katie is eager to learn French." He turned to the pastor. "If you have any questions, Michael will help you."

Michael bowed his head. "Yes, my lord." He then addressed the pastor and Katie. "If you two will follow me, I'll take you to the library."

The earl interrupted. "Oh yes, I will expect them in the formal dining room for the evening meal. They may get lost trying to get to their rooms to change for dinner. You will have to escort them."

Michael bowed his head. "I will see that they don't get lost."

When they left, the earl gestured towards Anna. "How about we take a walk in the gardens? It's lovely this time of year."

Anna smiled and nodded with her head. "That sounds like a wonderful idea. I have always loved beautiful gardens. Mine is small, but full of lilac bushes, roses, tulips." She paused. "To be honest, I have too many flowers and shrubs for such a small yard. But I couldn't decide what not to have. I love their beauty and fragrance. It seems that nature was meant to lift our spirits. In my backyard, I have a small gazebo where I sit in the afternoon on pleasant days and enjoy my flower garden."

Lord Cranston chuckled. "You sound like me. If I didn't have a thousand acres, I can't imagine what this place would look like with all the flowers and shrubs that I like." He stood up. "Well, let's go explore my gardens." He paused. "Of course, we'll probably not have time to see them all, but I want to show you my favorite. That's the one that I delight in sitting in and marveling at nature's beauty and fragrance."

When they walked through the entry into the the walled garden, Anna gasped. "This reminds me of the *Secret Garden* by

Frances Hodgson Burnett. It's what I would have expected it to look like. This is simply astonishing. I feel as though I've entered her story." She gestured towards the roses. "It's as if I can see Mary Lennox exclaiming about the roses. However, I never imagined how exquisite English roses can be. The color is so rich and vibrant." She paused. "Oh my, do you see the hummingbirds and butterflies all around the Veronica Bluestone?" She stood with her hands on her hips. "You have pink and blue Hydrangeas; the pH in your soil must be perfect." She placed both hands on her heart. "This place has made me almost forget about the Hercule Poirot mystery that we have been dealing with lately. It's like stepping into another world." She laughed. "Well, you have spoiled me. How will I ever be content with my little garden again? This is truly magnificent."

"I knew that you would say that. I sensed that we have a lot in common." He gestured with his right hand. "This garden was done under my complete supervision. It was what I envisioned the garden in Burnett's book to look like. You are the first one to ever suggest that." He walked over to a swing hanging from a sturdy oak branch. "Would you like to take a swing?"

Anna put her hands on her hips. "You must be reading my mind. I was thinking that I would love to take a swing on that. It's been years since I was on one." She sat on the wooden seat and chuckled. "I feel like a little girl again." She paused. "How strange things can become. I had given up a career in marketing at twenty-three to marry Daryl. My desire for children over rid my desire for a career. Besides neither of us believed that a wife or a husband should be travelling the country away from home. Now, at forty-six, I'm a widow without children and no career. I do thank God that Daryl had an insurance policy that was ample enough that I didn't have to try to find a job at forty-one. There's no excess, but I have always been frugal. I know what my budget is, and I stick to it." She laughed. "I believe that this truly is a secret garden. Listen to me divulging all my secrets. There is just such an overwhelming sense of the Lord in here that it's no place to keep secrets hidden. Confession is good for the soul."

The earl rubbed the back of his neck with his right hand. "I know what you mean. It's like I must confess what I have kept hidden for some time." He gave a heavy sigh. Matilda and I had a dream of filling Cranston Hall with children. We both desired at least four children." His eyes took on a haunted look. In the end, we had no children. Now, at fifty-nine, I'm a widower with no male heir. You see, even if I acknowledge Shirley as my daughter, she cannot be my heir. An heir must be male. Unless God performs a miracle like He did for Abraham and Sarah, my title and estate will go to my cousin Harry who is Joan's older brother. He also has two sons, so he has no problem with the heir issue." He gestured with his right hand. "The only thing that I can leave Shirley is my mother's estate of Hastings Manor in Darlington."

Anna chuckled. "It's a good thing Katie isn't hearing us talk. She might accuse us of being negative and reprimand the both of us for our lack of faith." She paused and gazed around. "But then again, her sensitivity to the Lord would see it as our receiving healing from Him." She gazed up at the earl. "Lord Cranston, as for an heir, when has anything ever been too difficult for God? I mean, after all, I'm sitting on a swing in an English Garden belonging to an earl. I'm sure that Hastings Manor must be a nice place to inherit. Just the name is quite intriguing."

He nodded. "You are quite right. It is rather an attractive manor with ten bedrooms, fifteen bathrooms, a huge conservatory facing the south and full of all kinds of herbs and plants. It has several parlors, an informal kitchen, a formal kitchen, and servants' quarters upstairs." He paused. "Hastings Manor is situated on Meadow Lake with two hundred and fifty acres of picturesque land. The grounds are quite lovely, but not like Cranston Hall." He grinned. "I'm rather partial to my birthplace. However, I always loved the manor. It's where my mother was born and grew up. Her grandmother's younger brother was only about ten years older than my mother. My great uncle Richard was always my favorite relative. I believe that I was closer to him than my father. It seemed that my father was always off on some sort of trip for this or that. I had vowed that when I got married that I would spend time with my wife and children." He gestured with his hands. "Hastings Manor has good memories."

"Well, I'm sure that I would think that Hastings Manor is lovely, but I believe that nothing can compare to Cranston Hall." She laughed. "When we rode up the first day, the three of us thought that we entered Pemberley in Jane Austen's novel. It was quite an overwhelming sight to behold. It was something to actually be in England, but to be the guest of an earl." She gestured with her hands. "Sitting in your secret garden has to be the epitome of this trip." She sighed. "I have not stopped thanking the Lord since I arrived here, and now this garden is overwhelming. I feel like I'll never be able to thank Him enough. This is a dream come true."

"Well, I thank God that I was able to make your dream a reality." He stared off as his countenance took on a thoughtful look.

7

FAITH KNOWS THAT
GOD IS ALWAYS GOOD

About a week later, Anna, Katie, Pastor Beaumont, and Lord Cranston all sat in his personal sitting room enjoying an afternoon cup of tea when Michael knocked on the door.

"Come in."

"My lord, Inspector Gauthier is here. Do you want me to bring him up here?"

Lord Cranston gestured with his right hand. "Yes, of course. We have been waiting to hear from him."

Michael ushered the inspector into the room and introduced him. "Inspector Gauthier."

"Thank you, Michael. You may leave us."

Gauthier gave a slight bow of his head towards Lord Cranston when Michael left the room. "My lord, we've identified prints belonging to a Normand Aubry Essex, Viscount Kildare."

Radcliffe's head went back, and his brows scrunched. "Are you quite sure?"

"*Ma foi.*"

"I'm aware of the viscount, but I only met him once about forty years ago. However, he's never attended any events since then." He gestured with his right hand. "Frankly, he's quite an elusive fellow. Has he been questioned?"

The inspector picked a piece of lint from his jacket. "Not yet, but we've notified the Royal Canadian Mounted Police."

"The Royal Canadian Mountain Police? Whatever for? What do they have to do with an English viscount?"

"Since his maternal grandfather left him a large legacy about forty years ago, the Viscount has spent most of his time at his inherited castle in Manitoba. He's rarely seen in public, even in Canada."

Anna felt her anxiety rise. "Wait a minute!" She took a deep breath. "Didn't you check to see if George Tyler's prints were on it? I mean, weren't his prints on it?"

Gauthier shook his head. "*Non, Madame.*" He straightened his suit coat. "The only prints found were yours, Shirley's, Lord Cranston's, the viscount's, and some too old to define."

Katie's eyebrows scrunched together. "Anna, I thought you said that George threw it away? If he touched it, why aren't his fingerprints on it?"

Anna fidgeted with her wedding band. "That's what Shirley told me." She gazed at the inspector. "Inspector Gauthier, are you telling us that George is this viscount?"

"*S'il vous plaît*, do not put the words in my mouth," he said and pointed up with his right forefinger. "All I'm saying is that Viscount Kildare's prints were on it."

Anna's mind reeled as she watched Gauthier straighten a picture on the wall. Were George and the viscount the same person? "Inspector, excuse me."

"*Oui.*"

"Do you have any pictures of the viscount?"

"Not recent ones, but the RCMP is wiring their most current ones." He straightened his tie and addressed the earl. "*Excusez-moi*, Lord Cranston, they are to be brought here as soon as they arrive. I didn't have time to inform you earlier, but I took the *liberté* to have them brought here. I felt it was *vital* to waste no time."

They were interrupted as Michael knocked on the door.

"Come in," the earl said.

"Excuse me, my lord, but there is a young man desiring to speak to the inspector."

"Let him in."

"Yes, my lord."

Michael let in a young man, who immediately spoke to Gauthier, while handing him an envelope. "Inspector, here are the viscount's photographs."

Gauthier took the contents out of the envelope, glanced at the pictures, handed them to Anna, and then dismissed the man. "Thank you for delivering them here. You may return to the Yard."

"T-this isn't George Tyler," Anna said, bewildered. "I've never seen this man before. I have no idea who he is." She paused. "Well, I mean, I know you said that he is the viscount, but I've never seen him before."

"Madame, you are sure?"

"Yes, I'm sure. I have no idea who this viscount is. He's a total stranger. This is becoming more of a mystery each day." Anna's eyebrows scrunched together. "I'm completely baffled. I mean, why didn't you find George's fingerprints on it? Shirley said that he threw it away. He couldn't have thrown something away without his fingers touching it."

Pastor Beaumont shook his head. "This gets more puzzling all the time. How did the viscount's prints get on Shirley's locket?" He gestured toward the earl. "Does she know the viscount?"

"I don't know how she could have met him. It's rather fantastic. I can think of no time that she may have encountered him. After all, I only met him once about forty years ago and he's a fellow aristocrat."

Katie looked at the pictures, twirled a curl with her forefinger and passed them to Lord Cranston. "Excuse me, but I was wondering if they've questioned the viscountess. Surely, she would know where he is."

"Lord Kildare isn't married," Gauthier said, adjusting his cuff links. "There's a rumor about a family curse. It seems that he won't marry because of the curse."

Lord Cranston appeared tense. "Well, he bloody well better elucidate how he knows Shirley."

"*Oui bon ami.* The viscount seems to have a lot to clarify. He pointed up with his right forefinger. "Now, all we have to do is locate him. He apparently spends most of his time in Canada. The Mounties are working on it as we speak."

Michael knocked on the door.

"Come in." When Michael entered, the earl spoke to him. "Michael, it seems that things are quite busy. If we have company in here with me, will you kindly knock once and just enter."

"Yes, my lord." He gave a slight bow with his head and addressed the inspector. "Excuse me inspector, but there is someone out here wishing to speak with you in private."

Gauthier turned to the earl. "*Pardon,* my lord." He gave a slight bow of his head. "Let me see what this is all about. I'll be back *dans un moment.*"

Katie watched the inspector leave the room and turned to the others. "This is a real mystery," she said, her jeweled eyes glittered. "Yet, at the same time, I sense the peace of the Lord. I can't explain it. All I know is that He's encouraging me to trust Him. Yet, I have no idea what I'm to trust Him with."

The pastor gave out a heavy sigh. "I just don't have a right feeling about this. It's a very uncomfortable sense that something is wrong." He paused and shook his head. "It's like the Lord keeps bringing my dream before my eyes. I believe that the Holy Spirit is trying to tell me something, but I don't understand it. All that I do know is that the Lord will reveal what it is that I don't comprehend when it's His time."

Anna felt her blood rush with foreboding. "I agree with you Matthew about something being wrong. I'm concerned that something dreadful has happened. I do feel the Lord's peace as Katie said, but I know there's something amiss."

Radcliffe rubbed his chin with his thumb and right forefinger. "I quite agree with the both of you. I'm having this unusual sensation that is like a great sadness. I can't explain it, but it is quite profound."

Pastor Beaumont scratched the back of his head with his left hand. "I don't remember ever having such a sense of foreboding in my whole life, I feel quite uncomfortable, but the Lord impresses me to trust Him." He gestured towards Katie. "I know what you mean. It's like the Lord is telling me to trust Him, but I don't really understand what for either." He gestured with both hands. I guess it doesn't matter what I understand. Faith trusts God no matter what is felt."

At that moment, Gauthier returned with a folder in his left hand. He seemed sullen, his face pallid. "The Royal Canadian Mounted Police have searched Kildare's castle." He paused to pick something off his jacket. "It appears that when the Mounties questioned the servants, one of the bed makers was confused as to how her lord always entered his chamber unnoticed." He pointed up with his right forefinger. "That told the Mounties there must be a secret entrance, and they went through his quarters with a fine-tooth bug rake to find it." He straightened his tie. "One of the fitted bookcases, covering the north wall, was actually a door to a hidden passage that led to a large underground cavern." He paused and looked at each face. "*C'est triste.*" He closed his eyes and gave out a heavy sigh. "The viscount must be batty. What the Mounties found in the rear of the cavern were concrete vaults, of which, four housed a body. In front of each vault, that contained a body, was a type of a marble shrine with a candle in a silver candlestick. In front of each candle was a picture of newlyweds encased in gold frames and in front of each picture there was a tiny crystal coffin with wedding bands." He then held up the folder. "These are copies of the couples." He gazed at the earl with dull eyes. "*Je Suis désolé*, but one of them is Joan Tyler, whose true identity is Shirley Radcliffe. It seems that the viscount murdered the women, but we have no idea who the men are. It seems that the coffins only housed the *femelle* and not the *male* in the pictures."

Pastor Beaumont felt a cold chill run through him as the Inspector spoke. "Inspector Gauthier, that's my dream. You explained every detail. Why would I dream about a man that I don't know? What can this be?"

The blood drained from Lord Cranston's face and his body went limp. "Oh my God! This can't be true." His eyes watered. "My Shirley's gone?" He said in a whisper.

Katie gazed at the pastor. "You did say about the shrines and things, but you also said something about me. I don't understand. I'm sitting here with all of you."

"Yes, but I said it felt like it would be the future. However, I now believe that it was to show that you would have been the next victim, that's why it couldn't focus in. But God has intervened to stop it from happening." He gestured with his hands. "It was not to take place."

Anna felt the strength of the Holy Spirit overtake her, and she reached over to give a gentle squeeze to the earl's forearm.

Pastor Beaumont bowed his head. "Please Lord, touch Lord Cranston with your peace that passes all understanding."

"*Pardon!*" Gauthier said. "Here are the pictures of the couples." He lined them up on the coffee table for all to see.

Anna looked at the pictures and screamed as black fright swept through her.

Katie ran to her side. "What happened? Are you ill?"

Anna, her heart pounding against her chest, cupped her mouth. "I feel sick." Gauthier seized the waste basket, and Radcliffe was jolted by her scream and handed her his silver canister. Anna took a sip and gasped as the brandy burned its way down her esophagus, then gave a demonstrative exhale. "I'm sorry," she said breathing through her nose and exhaling through her mouth several times. "I know all those couples! I'm telling you that I know every one of them." She pointed to each picture one at a time. "That's Bruce and Amanda Martin, that's Henry and Lily Cromwell, that's Charles and Connie Fitzborn and, of course, that's George and Joan Tyler."

"*Mon Dieu!*" Gauthier said. "How do you know them?"

She gestured toward Katie with her right hand. "They've all lived in Katie's house. Each couple has been my neighbor."

"Incredible!" Lord Cranston said as Inspector Gauthier dashed out of the room.

Katie's jeweled eyes widened. "I don't scare easily, but that's quite frightening. I mean, my house is where they all lived."

"This is even giving my faith a test," Pastor Beaumont said, scratching the back of his head with his left hand. "First my dream has me concerned about Katie, and now to find out that everyone who lived in her house prior to her is dead. Really, this is something from a suspense movie."

Katie shook her head. "I know what you mean. At first, I just felt it was like a mystery." She paused. "You mean this wouldn't fit into a Poirot mystery?"

"Well, maybe it would. Now that I think of it *The ABC Murders* could have been considered quite suspenseful." The pastor paused. "Yes, I guess it could have been a Poirot mystery."

"I'm not sure if the Lord wants me to go home after all of this, but I know that Byron will be back next month." Katie put her hair behind her ears with her fingers. "Maybe I can convince him that we cannot stay in that house. I mean, after I tell him all that has happened."

Anna sat, fidgeting with her wedding band. "Why did this man kill only my neighbors?"

"I know one thing," the earl said. "You two aren't leaving here until this is cleared up. We'll just have to let the police watch for Byron to come home and have him call Katie here." He gestured with his right hand. "I have grown quite fond of Katie's free-spirited nature." His eyes took on a haunted look. "I would have liked Shirley to have had more of Katie's personality, but she was always too solemn. Then after the diary was found, she seemed to lose any joy that she may have had."

Anna leaned forward in her chair. "That's what it was." She gestured with both hands. "Forgive me if I'm out of place. "But it was like joy wasn't in her vocabulary. No matter what it was, she was so serious. When other people would laugh, she just watched."

Lord Cranston gave out a heavy sigh. "She told me when she was about ten that a God that could take her mother before she ever knew her wasn't a very good God. I told her that God is always a good God whether we understand what is going on or not."

He sat back and folded his arms. "She was too young to understand about my wife and that I had no male heir, but that didn't mean that God wasn't good. We don't see what He sees or know what He knows."

Pastor Beaumont clapped his hands. "Amen, that's what faith is all about. It knows that God loves us and is always working on our behalf to get us to Heaven with Him. To put it simply, faith knows that God is always good."

Katie put her hair behind her ears with her fingers. "That's what Pastor Mitchell taught us at the orphanage. He always said that all things work together for good to them that love God, to them who are the called according to His purpose. We may not know what it is that God is doing, but we know that whoever loves Him will have everything work together for their good. He taught that the thing may not be good, but God will somehow in the end work it out for good. Besides, faith knows that God is always good." She gestured with her left hand toward the earl. "I thank you for your concern, but why should I start fearing man now? Faith in God has taken me this far and will see me through whatever is going on now." She giggled. "I confess that I enjoy the aristocratic lifestyle. To be honest, I read Jane Austen's novels over and over again, because I always daydreamed of being an aristocrat." She paused, and her eyebrows scrunched together. "The strangest part of it was that I had a dream where I believed the Lord told me that it wasn't a daydream. When I told Pastor Mitchell, he laughed and said that perhaps I should start to read some other books."

Pastor Beaumont stroked his jaw with his left hand. "All I know is that if it's only Anna's neighbors, there's definitely something sinister going on here."

Lord Cranston's eyes took on that haunted look. "And Anna you remind me so much of Joan in your looks, dress, and style. Yet, your personality is different. Now, that I think of it, Shirley was much like Joan. She also had no faith in the Lord. Her repentance wasn't for the Lord, but for Matilda. Although she took the shame to protect my reputation, I always knew that it was for Matilda." He sighed. "But as far as looks and style go, you and she could have been sisters." He gave a slow grin. "Truth be told, you are prettier and more stylish than Lady Joan was."

Anna rubbed the back of her neck with her right hand. "Shirley told me that I reminded her of a picture of a Lady Joan. She never told me anything about the picture or where she saw it. I just remember the first time that I met her, she gave a gasp and went back. She laughed and shrugged it off and said it was like she was looking at a picture that she had seen."

"It was her mother that she used to stare at for hours when she was younger. She always remarked that she wished that she looked like her mother, but she didn't know who she looked like." He sighed. "I never had the nerve to tell her that she looked like my mother's grandmother. She never saw her or any pictures of when she was young."

Anna fidgeted with her wedding band. "I'm glad that I had the time with her that I did. Now, that I know she never knew her mother makes me happy that she felt that I resembled that picture. Perhaps, it gave her five years of seeing her mother through me." She sighed. "I did always tell her about the goodness of the Lord." She looked at Pastor Beaumont. "You remembered that she did attend church with me several times after Daryl died." She turned her attention toward the earl. "Pastor Beaumont remembered that there were tears in her eyes when he preached on God's love. I pray that faith took root in her. God is able to save to the utmost."

"Anna, I thank you for that. It is most comforting." He rubbed his chin with his right forefinger and thumb. "I believe that the Lord may have touched her heart with His love."

8

Light Exposes What's Hidden in the Darkness

Anna, Katie, Pastor Beaumont, and Lord Cranston sat in his personal sitting room when the butler announced the arrival of Inspector Gauthier.

"Please, show him in."

"Yes, my lord," Michael said.

When the inspector entered the room, the earl gestured with his right hand towards a double chair settee to the right of Anna. "Have a seat."

Gauthier brushed something off the seat and sat down. "My lord," he said with a quick bow of his head, "Viscount Kildare has committed a *mort volontaire*."

Katie gasped. "Why would he kill himself?"

Anna almost dropped her cup of tea. "Was he the killer? Why else would he kill himself?"

"Because of a hush, I've not been given the details. However, Canada has sent someone who has the answers. He turned toward Lord Cranston. "I've taken the *liberté* to give consent for him to meet me here instead of the yard. I felt that no time should be *perdu*."

The earl motioned with both hands. "That is quite all right. I really wish to get to the bottom of this grief. You did well in having him meet you here, so that we can all hear what he has to say."

Before the inspector could respond, Michael knocked once and let a strange man into the room. He genuflected toward the earl. "I'm Jeffrey Crevier from the RCMP's national headquarters in Ottawa, Ontario. I've been sent by the Commissioner's Office to speak in person." He paused and eyed each of them individually before going on. "It's been affirmed that Lord Kildare was the killer."

Anna gasped. "Where did he bury the men? Why didn't he bury them with their wives?"

Jeffrey gestured for her to be calm. "Let me continue. I will take one thing at a time and all should become reasonably clear." He motioned towards the inspector with his right hand. "Have you informed them of the viscount's suicide?"

"*Oui*. I just finished telling them before you came in."

"Good, then I will continue. Apparently, he must have seen the surveillance and knew his time was up. He went to his solicitor and gave him an envelope to be opened upon his death. In it were the identifications of all the men, a full confession, and an amendment to his latest will." He fixed his eyes on Katie. "Certain factors have been held back, because the Commissioner felt it proper decorum that Mrs. Mathers be informed of everything before it's released to the media."

Katie's eyebrows squished together. "Did something happen to Byron?"

Anna grabbed Katie's right hand. "I believe that Mr. Crevier is saying that the viscount and Byron were one and the same." She glared at Crevier. "I am correct in saying that; am I not?"

"That is quite right. However, I'm also saying that the viscount was all the men in the pictures."

"Shocking!" Cranston exclaimed.

"That is what I expected," Gauthier said as he adjusted his cufflink.

"Then it was the viscount that I saw in my dream. The candle lights made it difficult for me to make out his face." Matthew scratched the back of his head with his left hand. "It was because he was going to kill Katie next that the Lord gave me that dream. That's why we were all together when the news of Shirley appeared. The Lord wanted Katie to be here when this all came out."

"That's what I believe," Anna sighed.

Pastor Beaumont clasped his hands. "That's what the Lord meant when he told Katie that He was about to bring to light what had been hiding in darkness." He gestured with his left hand towards Katie. "His light has kept you from harm."

Jeffrey Crevier put up his hand to still them all and continued. "In his confession, the viscount wanted you to know that you were his favorite and wished it could've been different. You were going to be number five, but a doctor's visit three months ago revealed that he had only six months to a year to live. It seems that he was getting prepared to admit who he was to Katie, when the surveillance was discovered." He paused. "When he went to the doctor's last week, the cancer had spread so rapidly that he only had about a month to live." He scratched the back of his head with his right hand. "Although he's officially claimed his marriage to you, his Kildare estate is entailed to the nearest male relative. However, Aubry Castle in Manitoba and his maternal grandfather's legacy has been left to you. He has left you a very wealthy young lady."

Katie's jeweled eyes seemed troubled. "Sir are you sure it's Byron Mathers?"

Jeffrey shook his head. "I'm sorry Mrs. Mathers, but it has been affirmed. There is no doubt that the viscount and your husband were one and the same."

Anna reached over and touched Katie's right hand. "Katie, like Matthew said, you were told by the Lord when you read Psalm 112 that He was about to bring to light what has been hidden in darkness. He has done what He promised. You have to trust His word to you."

"We must trust Him," Pastor Beaumont interjected. "He has saved your life. Byron said that you were to be number five. I mean, really, how dark could this guy have been?"

Lord Cranston sat back and folded his arms. "This is all rather shocking to say the least." He gave out a heavy sigh. "Not to change the subject, but what does all this mean? Will the viscount have a funeral?"

Jeffrey nodded his head and turned to Katie. "Mrs. Mathers, I have made all the arrangements for you to come with me to Canada. It seems that you must be at the reading of his will."

"One blooming minute," Lord Cranston interrupted. "I believe that Anna, Pastor Beaumont, and I will accompany Katie to Canada. Does the Commissioner have any problems with us attending?"

Jeffrey smiled. "My lord, I think that she would be pleased to make your acquaintance. It would probably be easier for Mrs. Mathers to have friends with her. This has all been a shock to her."

Katie's emerald eyes sparkled. "Mr. Crevier, I don't know where you stand in the faith category, but my faith in the Lord has seen me through much in my short life. I trust that He will be my help through this." She flushed and gestured toward Anna, Pastor Beaumont, and Lord Cranston. "That doesn't mean that I don't want all of you to accompany me. I will be quite pleased if you do. To be honest, I feel rather weird attending a funeral of a husband that seems to be a total stranger. I have no idea who he really was." She twirled a curl with her left forefinger. "When I saw the pictures of the other four men and the viscount, I saw no resemblance to Byron." She gestured with her hands. "I'm totally flabbergasted that one man could be six different men. Perhaps, when I see the man in the coffin, I'll see a likeness." She shook her head. "It's not that I doubt what was said, but it is quite bizarre that a man can appear to be six different men."

Crevier gestured with both hands. "I will answer your question about faith. I'm not sure what I personally think. However, I have always admired anyone who can have it. It does seem to give them strength under very dire circumstances that's beyond my understanding. In fact, there have been times that I have wished that I had that kind of faith to help me through."

Katie's jeweled eyes sparkled. "Anyone who believes in Jesus as Lord can have faith. It's that simple. There's no complex way to faith; it's as simple as asking Jesus to be your Lord and trusting in God's love for you. Once you understand that God's love for you sent Jesus to die on the cross for your sins, it does something inside your heart. It overwhelmed me with love for Jesus to think that He suffered that horrible death on the cross for me. That's when I knew that I wanted Him to be my Lord." She gestured with both hands. "I did that at the age of ten, and He has been lighting up my life through thick and thin for sixteen years."

The pastor leaned forward in his seat. "Wow! I was ten years of age when I accepted him as savior. That's incredible!"

Lord Cranston rubbed his chin with his right forefinger and thumb. "This is getting rather remarkable. I, too, was ten when my mother led me to the Lord." He gestured towards Anna. "Well, Anna, that leaves you. It's obvious that you know the Lord, but since what age?"

Anna fidgeted with her wedding band. "I was just sitting here somewhat fascinated as I listened to you all. My mind went back to my grandmother taking me to a revival meeting when I was ten. I went to the altar and asked Jesus to be my savior. He's been my Lord ever since."

Pastor Beaumont scratched the back of head with his left hand. "This is all incredible. Only the Lord could have brought the four of us together." He gestured with his left hand. "Let's face it. What are the odds of four people in one room all being saved at ten years of age? God is so awesome."

§

Katie, Anna, Pastor Beaumont, and Lord Cranston flew to Canada with Jeffrey Crevier to attend the private funeral for the viscount and the reading of his will. Anna prayed that when Katie saw the body that the resemblance would be obvious.

Katie's eyes widened, and her mouth dropped opened as she viewed the man in the casket. Jeffrey helped her to her seat. "I'm very sorry Mrs. Mathers. I beg your pardon, I mean, Lady Kildare."

Katie's voice cracked. "This is all so surreal. I feel as though I should wake up from all this and find myself home." She gestured with her left hand. "You see, I know that it's Byron. The profile is the same; there's no mistake about it. But it's hard to believe that such a kind man could really be a Dr. Jekyll and Mr. Hyde. The only man that I knew was the Jekyll. He never lost his temper or did anything that would have given me a clue that he could be a Hyde. It's so unbelievable, but I know that it's the truth." She paused and twirled a curl with her left forefinger. "But you know what? I believe that this is another one of those thick and thin things that the Lord has brought me through. The only reason that I married Byron is because I thought it was the Lord giving me Isaac and Rebekah. Now, I know it wasn't. I am ashamed that I never really prayed it through." She grabbed her heart with both hands. "I don't understand why the Lord protected my presumption. He truly protected me from harm. It is so bewildering to find out that I married a murderer who would have murdered me next." She paused. "However, I remember Pastor Mitchell saying that God is omniscient; there isn't anything that He doesn't know. He knew what Byron, or the viscount was, but He also knew that I was not going to be his next victim. Because of everything that God knew, He made it possible for all of us to be in England."

Pastor Beaumont scratched the back of his head with his left hand. "Yes, but the Lord told you that your dream to be an aristocrat was not a daydream. It was his will for you." He paused. "I believe that the Lord allowed you to think what you thought about Isaac and Rebekah so that He could move you across the street from Anna. Otherwise, you would not be here today." He gave a heavy sigh. "Of course, I wouldn't recommend anyone marrying because they thought something and never prayed it through. Just because He protected you doesn't mean that someone else would be protected. God knew what you would do, so He allowed it to bring about His promise."

Suddenly Katie's jeweled eyes widened. "Wait a minute! Did you just call me Lady Kildare? Is that what I heard?"

"In the will, to be read shortly, he officially claims the marriage," Jeffrey said, a trace of laughter in his voice. "It seems that you are Lady Kildare until death, unless you marry another peer."

Lord Cranston rubbed his chin with his right forefinger and thumb. "Well, my dear, you can no longer call yourself a commoner. Your title is probably one of courtesy, but it will be recognized by your fellow aristocrats." He reached out to shake her hand with his right hand. "May I personally welcome you as a member of the aristocracy? It gladdens my heart to have something good come out of all this sadness."

Katie jumped up. "Matthew, that's why you mentioned my dream to be an aristocrat not being a daydream; it was the Lord's will." She giggled. "I don't want to wake up from this dream. I feel sad about Byron or the viscount, but I'm too excited at what God has done to let sadness interfere with this miracle." She put her hair behind her ears with her fingers. "I'm overwhelmed with such excitement that I want to jump up and down and shout God's praises."

Anna cupped Katie's face with her hands. "I knew that I wasn't meant to be a typical mother."

Pastor Beaumont stood up, grabbed his chest with both hands, and practically fell back into his chair.

Lord Cranston handed him his silver canister. "Please take a swallow of this."

"No." He put up his hands. "I'm all right." He gave out a heavy sigh and touched Lord Cranston's right arm. "I just saw Anna pregnant with your heir." He paused. "The Lord said that his name is Richard Ansbury Radcliffe. I have no idea what that means."

Anna gasped. "Ansbury is my maiden name, but I don't know any Richard."

The earl took on a haunted look. "I always said that I wanted my heir to be named after my great uncle Richard Ansbury. He was the brother of my grandmother whose maiden name was Ansbury." He turned toward Anna. "As I was saying this, the Lord said that you will become with child on our honeymoon." He grinned. "Well, Anna what do you say?"

"Anna's eyes filled with tears. "I'm beside myself with joy. I will gladly be your wife." She paused. "Does that mean that I'm to be an aristocrat?"

Katie chuckled. "Well, Anna if you are married to an earl, that will make you a countess." She turned to the earl. "I studied all the titles when I was doing my daydreaming."

Lord Cranston stood and kneeled before Anna. "Let's do this properly." He took her right hand in his. "Anna Ansbury Paquette, will you be my wife?"

"Yes, a thousand times yes." She stood with her hands on her hips. "God has been using this whole time for confessions. When Shirley said that I reminded her of a Lady Joan, it was not the first time that I had been told that I had the appearance of a Lady. My mother died when I was very young, and my grandmother raised me. She always called me Lady Anna." Anna gestured with her right hand. "My grandmother wanted me to know that I was born to be someone special."

Lord Cranston cupped Anna's right hand in his hands. "You have made me a very happy man. I am humbled at God's blessing. I am quite overwhelmed by His goodness." He cleared his throat. "Next month is August, and I would love to be married on my mother's birthday. So, if you are willing, we could make the eighth of August our wedding day."

Anna placed her left hand on top of his left hand. "Lord Cranston, everything is so incredible; the eighth of August was my mother's birthday."

He gave a slow grin. "There seems to be a slight impediment in all this."

Anna's eyebrows scrunched together. "There is? W-what do you mean?"

"It appears that an upcoming wife should call her future husband by his name. If you would be so considerate, would you kindly address me as William?"

Anna stretched out her right hand. "Yes, William, I can accommodate you."

Katie giggled. "Well, now it seems that I will have a little brother." She twirled a curl around her left forefinger. "I truly wish you two were my parents." Her eyes filled with tears. "I could not have hoped for a better father and mother."

The earl took Katie's right hand. "I think that we both would love to adopt you as our daughter. We will start the legal proceedings and make it official right after our wedding."

9

GOD MAKES ALL THINGS BEAUTIFUL IN HIS TIME

Anna and Lord Cranston were talking about their upcoming wedding when the earl addressed her about her personal belongings in America. "We will definitely have to retrieve your personal property from Hunts Grove. It would be more convenient if I send some staff to retrieve them."

Anna fidgeted with her wedding band. "I have a lot of antiques, but I won't need them here. There are a few that belonged to my grandmother's mother that I am especially fond of. I will describe them and say where they are located. Outside of those few items, my grandmother's silver tea set, and my personal effects, that should be it." She gestured with her right hand to Pastor Beaumont. "Matthew, do you know of anyone who the Lord would want to bless with my home and furniture? I feel that the Lord wants me to give it to someone, but I do not know to whom."

Matthew fell back in his seat and clasped his hands together. "Yes, I do. One of the deacons in the church and his wife lost their house last year. He had an accident and was unable to walk for almost a year. They went into debt with medical bills and such and they couldn't keep up the mortgage payment. James and his wife Deborah both said that the Lord was in charge of their life and trusted that whatever God was doing would be for their good.

They believe that God makes all things beautiful in His time." He held back tears. "I'm beside myself with elation for them. They have remarkable faith."

"God is so good." Anna said. "This is just like Him to bless me so that I can bless others."

Lord Cranston took Anna's right hand in his. "I believe that it will be my turn to bless someone next. At present, I don't know who or with what, but I feel it rather keenly."

Jeffrey Crevier stood up. "Excuse me, but it is time for the reading of the will. If you will all follow me, I will take you to the solicitor who is waiting."

They all followed to a large room set up with chairs. In the front of the room at a mahogany table sat a rather stocky man in his early sixties with wire rimmed spectacles. He gestured to the chairs. "If you would please be seated, we can get on with this. I don't mean to rush, but I have an important appointment later this afternoon that I cannot be late for." He perused the group and paused at Katie. "I'm Eugene Mullens, the viscount's solicitor, and you must be Mrs. Mathers. Am I correct?"

Katie nodded. "Yes, I am Mrs. Mathers."

He picked up the papers that were on the table in front of him. "Okay, let's proceed." He read where Normand Aubrey Essex, the Viscount Kildare admitted his crimes. He revealed that Katie would have been number five, but his doctor's visit the month before revealed that he had about a month to live. He didn't have time to get to Katie to tell her who he was, because the pain had become unbearable. When he saw the surveillance at the castle, he knew that he had been discovered. It talked about the family curse, and his plan to outwit it. He believed that God would forgive him, since he was overcoming a curse on his family. He recognized Katie as Katherine Essex, Viscountess Kildare. Aubry Castle in Manitoba was left to her, his entire maternal grandfather's legacy and his property in Hunts Grove. His estate in England would fall to his nearest male relative, as well as the title of Viscount Kildare. By the time Mr. Mullens finished, everyone sat somewhat stunned. It was Pastor Beaumont that spoke first. "I know what he did was irrational, but he must have been quite tormented in his soul hiding such a dark secret."

Anna fidgeted with her wedding band. "I think that I'm somewhat confused. It talks about a family curse, but what was the curse?"

Mr. Mullens answered. "I'm aware of the curse, as I have known the family for years. My father was the family solicitor before me." He sat back in his chair. "It's really a sad tale, especially now that we know that Normand did what he did. You see, it seems a tale started about a family curse that caused four of the last viscounts to die shortly after their fifth anniversary leaving young widows and very young children." He gave out a heavy sigh. "Normand heard this from a child, and his fear turned into an unbelievable scheme to master the curse by overdosing his wives with opioids on their fifth anniversary." He paused. "That is what he did to himself rather than face the law for his crimes. Anyway, he believed in his confused state of mind that he could beat the so-called curse."

He gazed at them. "If there are no further questions, I will leave you for now." He handed Katie some papers. "These are copies of everything that you'll need. It's his will and all the necessary papers revealing that you own Aubry Castle in Manitoba, that you have inherited his entire maternal grandfather's legacy and that you are legally the widow of Normand Aubrey Essex, Viscount Kildare." He put out his right hand. "It's a pleasure to meet you, Lady Kildare as I will be handling all your legal matters. All my information is included in the papers; you may contact me at any time." He turned to pick up his briefcase. "Now, if you will excuse me, I will bid you all good day."

Anna felt her pulse quicken. "Katie! That's why he said that you would do something special before your fifth anniversary. He must have planned the something special to ease his conscience."

Katie's mouth dropped, and her jeweled eyes widened. "That's what he was going to do to me. He would have taken me on a cruise or a European tour that somehow docked in Canada, and then taken me to the cavern under the castle. I guess he would have given me the overdose of opioids before."

Pastor Beaumont stroked his jaw with his left hand. "Yes, he may have planned many things, but cancer stopped him from ever coming close to fulfilling his plan for you. God told you He would bring to light what has been hidden in darkness." He sat back and threw up his hands. "Don't you see how the devil was elated that you married Byron thinking that he would get rid of a Christian. However, God used the evil and turned it into good to fulfill his promise to you about being an aristocrat?" He paused. "I realize that you are not an actual aristocrat in the fact that your title is probably a courtesy, but you have inherited a castle and a large legacy. Besides, you will be called the Lady Kildare." He chuckled. "Wow! God is awesome."

Lord Cranston took Katie's right hand. "This has been an ordeal for me, but I am so thankful to the Lord for protecting you. I have grown very fond of you. You remind me so much of my mother. She had the same bubbly personality and was full of faith in the Lord. She would have taken to you. It's only fitting that you should be our daughter." He paused. "I have only one request. I know that your name is Katherine, but would you mind taking the name of Katherine Louise? My mother's name was Louise."

Katie giggled. "That will be quite easy, since my name is Katherine Louise."

Matthew Beaumont scratched the back of his head with his left hand. "I mean this trip has revealed so much. First, I find that Anna was married to my second cousin, when I thought that I had no family left. Then we all realize that we accepted the Lord as savior at ten years of age. Then we find out what God meant when He said that He would reveal what was hidden in darkness. Next, Katie comprehends that God really intended for her to be an aristocrat. Now, it is revealed that Lord Cranston will have his heir, and that Anna will also be an aristocrat. Plus, Katie's name is really Katherine Louise." He paused. "Oh yes, Lord Cranston's mother and Anna's mother both have the same birthday." He paused, sat back in his chair, and stared straight ahead.

Katie touched his shoulder. "Matthew, are you okay? You look strange."

"The Lord said that my wife is ready to marry me." He stood up and took Katie's right hand. "Are you ready?"

Katie grabbed her heart with her left hand and flopped into the chair. "I thought it was me. For months, I have been having dreams that we were getting married. I rebuked the devil, because I was married to Byron." She gestured with both hands. It's just that we seem to have so much in common. We both love the Lord, our sensitivity to His Holy Spirit, and just about everything." She bowed her head, prayed, and then gazed at Matthew. "I do love you and believe that my dreams were the Lord preparing me. However, I'm somewhat confused again. I believed that when I was about sixteen that the Lord said that my husband would be an artist. Byron wasn't interested in any kind of art."

Matthew asked Jeffrey Crevier if he had a pencil and paper. "Yes, I have my notebook and a pencil." He tore out a piece of paper, handed it to Matthew along with his pencil.

They all watched as he gazed at Katie and hastily wrote on the paper. "Here, I think that this should take away any confusion."

"Oh my," Katie giggled. "It's me. Why didn't you tell us you were an artist?"

"It never came up. We've always been so busy with things to do." Matthew scratched the back of his head with his left hand. "A few years ago, the Lord told me that He was going to change my life so that I could pursue my heart's desire of art. I know that art is my natural gift and ability from God. It's like I preach sermons through my art. However, I've never had the time to do what's in my heart to do. I knew that I was to preach, but I love art. God had told me that I was called to preach for a season. He made it clear that I was to remain single as a preacher like the apostle Paul, but I would be married as an artist. He told me to remember Amos." He gestured with his hands. "I never understood what was meant by Amos, but I just trusted Him to make things clear in His time."

"Dear me!" Anna interrupted. "Now I know what bothered me about that house. I know that I said that it was strange that each couple moved away before five years, because each husband always received a sudden promotion that moved them quickly. It was a cycle. I mean after the second time, I should have realized that if it happened again something was wrong." She gave out a heavy sigh. "I believe that I picked up on the cycle, but I could never put the pieces together."

Jeffrey looked puzzled. "What I don't understand is how you didn't recognize any similarity in the men's voices? I mean he must have given some hint of his identity after five times."

Anna shook her head. "You don't understand, I never talked to any of them. It did trouble me that they completely avoided me. But the wives all befriended me, so I decided that the husbands weren't the friendly type. The wives all stated that because their husband worked with so many people on the job, they just wanted peace and quiet when they were home. That sounded reasonable to Daryl and me." She put her hands on her hips. "What really baffles me is that I never saw any resemblance in any of the husbands. They truly looked like five different men. How did he disguise himself so effectively?" She gestured towards Katie. "Katie saw the resemblance of the viscount and Byron, but I never saw any similarity with any of them."

Jeffrey sat back and folded his arms. "What I was told is that he dyed his hair, styled it differently, or shaved it off. His eye color was changed with contacts. Sometimes, he'd wear glasses, grow a beard, or grow a moustache. One time he'd lose weight and the next time he'd gain it. Whatever person he played would determine his style of dress and his manner of walk. He even changed his mannerisms for each person he claimed to be. He had it down to a science and never altered from who he was supposed to be at the time." Jeffrey Crevier glanced uneasily at Katie. "It seems that Viscount Kildare was a master of disguise. That's why he was able to go near the castle and the surveillance didn't recognize him. Once he was aware that his time was up, he went to England and finalized everything with Mr. Mullens. He walked into his office undetected by anyone who was looking for the viscount. When Mr. Mullens questioned him about the disguise, Normand said that he didn't like publicity. He found it easier to move around while disguised. Since Mr. Mullens knew that he was not one for public events, he accepted his explanation without question. After all, he had no idea the man that had walked into his office was supposed to be Byron Mathers."

Lord Cranston rubbed his chin with his right forefinger and thumb. "I still don't understand how this went undetected for so long. I mean, there were coffins in that cavern. Surely, someone must have been trying to find their loved one."

Jeffrey shook his head. "My lord, all the wives except Shirley had no loved ones. Each one was an orphan without any family connections who would never be missed. He had no idea that Shirley had any family. From what they learned from evidence at Aubry Castle, the viscount believed that all the women were orphans with no family. He counted on no one ever knowing about them." He gestured with his right hand. "If they had no family, no one would be trying to find them. He had five years to make sure that they had no communication with anyone. Apparently, he wasn't concerned about his neighbors in Hunts Grove."

Katie twirled a curl with her finger. "This is really confusing. Why didn't he just marry as the viscount? Why did he continue the entire charade?"

Pastor Beaumont interjected. "I believe that I know why. If he married as the viscount, that would have made national news. Deception hid his intentions. Remember, he believed that there was a family curse from a young boy. He must have planned for years how to beat the curse." He paused. "My only question is what would he have done if he had a male heir?"

"In that case," Jeffrey answered, "he would have recognized the marriage so that his heir would be next in line. Then I believe that his wife would have had a sudden illness or something before their fifth anniversary."

Anna breathed heavily. "I just wish that I had paid closer attention to him. Maybe I could have recognized a resemblance."

Pastor Beaumont took her right hand. "You must trust the Lord. If you were supposed to see something, you would have done so." He gestured towards Katie. "Remember, the Lord told Katie that He was going to bring to light what was hidden in the darkness? He didn't tell you that."

Anna smiled. "Between you and Katie, I keep being brought into the right perspective. You are right. I guess it was because of Shirley that I was thinking that I wished I had seen something."

Lord Cranston rubbed his chin with his right forefinger and thumb. "Anna, I don't blame you for not seeing something. I saw those pictures of the men, and I would never have believed that they were the same person." He gestured towards Pastor Beaumont. "Like the pastor told me, Shirley knew that I was her father. I realize that she chose to leave instead of staying. I told her that I loved her and would acknowledge her legally, but she just became so angry and left." He took Anna's right hand. "It is apparent that all of it was God's plan to bring you into my life. I don't understand it, but I believe that God was working good out of all this evil."

Pastor Beaumont threw up his hands. "I understand! I mean about Amos the prophet. You see, he was a not a prophet, but a shepherd working with the herd when God called him to prophesy to Israel. It seems that he went forth and delivered the message that God gave him and when he finished, he went back to his herd." He gestured with both hands. "What I'm saying is that I wanted to do sermons through art showing the goodness of God to us, but the Lord said that I was to preach the Word until my wife was ready and then be like Amos. Now, I understand it, I'm to go back to my art when we marry."

Katie giggled. "I don't know if any of you remember that Sunday school taught us the potter takes the broken pieces of clay and makes them into something beautiful. I believe that God is taking all the broken pieces in our lives and turning them into something beautiful just like that couple that is going to get Anna's house." She flushed. "Not that preaching is broken pieces." She gestured with her left hand. "But not having any family can leave one somewhat broken."

Matthew grinned. "I must admit that at times I did wish that I had a family." He gestured to Katie and Anna. "However, once we started the Monday fried chicken and potato salad at Anna's, I felt that I had a family."

Katie threw up her hands. "Oh my, I'll have to give the house in Hunts Grove away. As far as personal belongings, there are just a few things that the staff can easily put in a suitcase. To be honest, I really want to forget about being Mrs. Mathers." She gestured at Matthew. "Do you know anyone who God would want to bless with my house?"

"As a matter of fact, I do believe that the youth pastor and his family would be God's choice. Philip and Priscilla Andrews have worked selflessly for the Lord and would love to have their own home. Philip will be so elated to have the pastoral position and a new home. There will be no problem for him to be voted in to the position." He clasped his hands together. "God makes all things beautiful in His time."

Jeffrey's eyebrows scrunched together. "That's quite profound. I've watched and listened to all of you during this ordeal. I must admit that it seems that your faith is giving strength that quite astonishes me." He grinned. "Perhaps it's time that I went back to church."

At that moment a man came up to Jeffrey. "Sir, everything is ready for the viscountess to come to the castle."

"Does that mean that his mistress is gone?"

"Yes, sir. Mademoiselle Barbette was informed that he has left everything to his wife and formerly named Mrs. Mathers as the wife of the Viscount Kildare." He handed Crevier a piece of paper. "If you will excuse me, the Commissioner is expecting me back."

While Jeffrey was reading the paper, Lord Cranston interrupted. "Excuse me, did you ask about his mistress?"

"Yes, I did. His paramour lived at Aubry Castle. She was his cover up. Anyone who knows the viscount is aware of the curse. They were all convinced that he took the mistress, so he didn't have to get married."

Anna fidgeted with her wedding band. "I still don't understand why he didn't marry as the viscount. Yes, you said it would have made the news. But it doesn't make sense."

"He figured that marrying like he did would hide his intentions. A Lady Kildare would have been out in public. People would have been watching all their travels and whatever. Who would be paying attention to a small middle-class neighborhood in America? Apparently, all he wanted was a male heir." He paused. "You see, in the cavern was a diary. In it, he begged God for an heir. If God would give him an heir, then he would not marry anyone else. If he had been given a son, he would've sold the Hunt's Grove house, taken the cruise, confessed his identity, claimed his son as heir, and then made sure the wife had some sort of accident prior to their fifth anniversary."

Lord Cranston rubbed his chin with his right forefinger and thumb. "I can understand wanting an heir, but to go to such extreme measures is quite sad. His hidden secret must have surely tormented his soul."

Katie twirled a curl around her left forefinger. "Boy, this gets more unbelievable all the time. Now, I must admit that does bother me that he had a mistress. I really thought that he believed in the Lord and His Word." She gazed at Jeffrey. "Are you saying that she lives at the castle?"

"Not anymore, she has left and all her belongings. You see some from Mr. Mullens office have been there getting things done, and the servants are eager to accommodate the viscountess." He paused. "When all this came out, Mademoiselle Barbette confessed that she was not a real mistress. She was paid quite handsomely to play the part of the mistress. Her bank account verifies her claim. It seems that her rooms were at the other end of the castle. But when he was there, she would go to his quarters. It was to give the appearance of what was not going on. Apparently, the viscount would not have any relation outside of marriage. She had no idea that he was such a troubled man. He told her that he wanted people to leave him alone until he found someone that he wanted to marry." He gestured with his hands. "It seems his mistress was one in name only and not in reality. She loved the prestige and the money, so went along with it."

Anna's eyebrows scrunched together. "What about the cavern? Are the shrines still there?"

"All the bodies were removed to a formal graveyard, except Shirley Montgomery's." Jeffrey turned toward the earl. "My lord, her body will be sent to England to be buried in the Cranston burial grounds, as you requested."

Lord Cranston's eyes took on a haunted look. "Thank you. I knew that Shirley would come home, but I didn't think it would be this way." He gave out a heavy sigh. "At least I won't be wondering where she is." His eyes watered. "Her gravestone will say that she is the beloved daughter of William Hastings Radcliffe, Earl of Cranston."

Jeffrey gestured toward Katie with his right hand. "Lady Kildare, there is no trace of the shrines or any foul play. Everything has been seen to, and the cavern is in its original condition."

"Well," Cranston said. "I've never been relieved that someone is dead before, but I'm glad the viscount can no longer carry out his charade."

Anna hung her head. "I know what you mean." She took Katie's right hand. "I'm so grateful to the Lord that you are still here."

"I quite agree," Pastor Beaumont interjected. "I believe it is as Katie said that the Lord is taking the broken pieces and making them whole."

Jeffrey's forehead wrinkled. "But I hope that Lady Kildare doesn't identify the viscount's mental illness with the castle. Aubry Castle is a magnificent place. I can see why he spent so much time there." He paused. "The only concern seems to be the servants who are hoping that the viscountess will retain them."

"I've never been a superstitious person. If they are doing their job, they may keep them." Katie's eyebrows scrunched together. "To be honest, I'm struggling with this whole thing. I really don't want to live on another continent that far from Lord Cranston and Anna." She twirled a curl around her left forefinger. "Unless Matthew wants to, I would rather sell it and live in England."

Matthew scratched the back of head with his left hand. "I guess this is confession time. If I had my choice, I would rather live in England." He gestured with his hands. "I've grown quite fond of Lord Cranston and Anna. Besides, I don't wish to be on a different continent either."

Katie giggled. "I told you that we have a lot in common."

Lord Cranston rubbed his chin with his right forefinger and thumb. "Well, I believe that I now know who I am to bless and with what. I was going to leave Hastings Manor in Darlington to Shirley. It was my mother's estate, and it's only about an hour from Cranston Hall. I do believe that you two would be quite pleased to have it." He paused. "However, since money doesn't seem to be a problem with you inheriting his maternal grandfather's estate, I wouldn't sell Aubry Castle. We could all spend certain holidays or whatever at it. It might be a nice get away from the jostle and flurry that can sometimes be England. The castle is in the upper part of Bathton and far away from any populated area."

Katie's jeweled eyes sparkled. "You said that I reminded you of your mother. I would be honored to be given her estate." She giggled. "I really like the name of Hastings Manor. It sounds regal."

Matthew nodded. Yes, I know I will be pleased to be able to live in England." He grinned. "Hastings Manor does sound quite noble. I'm so overwhelmed by God's goodness that I believe that I'm in a state of euphoria."

Katie twirled a curl around her left forefinger. "I think that I'm in the same state of total joy in the Lord." She paused. "Come to think of it, I do believe that it would be a good idea to keep the castle for vacations." She giggled. "I think that some of the English aristocracies have castles in Scotland. Ours will be in Canada."

Anna rubbed the back of her neck with her right hand. "I feel as though I just entered into a dream, but I know that I'm awake." She smiled. "I just pinched myself and it hurt."

They all laughed at that and the earl responded. "I rather believe that we all could feel that we have entered into a wonderful dream."

Matthew Beaumont clasped his hands. "This is God giving us the desires of our heart. He has taken all of the past brokenness and made something beautiful for the future."

Lord Cranston's voice cracked with emotion. "God truly does make all things work out for good to those who love Him."

"Amen!" Anna exclaimed.